get busy living...

Dedicated to every kid who has ever had trouble with reading comprehension—

It is my hope that this book can help you turn the page on that struggle.

...or get busy frying.

The Lexile Framework® for Reading

The Lexile Framework® for Reading (www.Lexile.com) is a scientific approach to measuring reading ability and the difficulty of reading materials. The Lexile Framework includes a Lexile® measure and the Lexile scale. A Lexile measure represents both the difficulty of a text, such as a book or article, and an individual's reading ability. Lexile measures are expressed as numeric measures followed by an "L" (e.g., 850L), and are placed on the Lexile scale. The Lexile scale is a developmental scale for measuring reader ability and text difficulty, ranging from below 200L for beginning readers and beginning-reader materials to above 1700L for advanced readers and materials. Knowing the Lexile measures of a reader and text helps to predict how the text matches the reader's ability—whether the text may be too easy, too difficult or just right. All Lexile products and services rely on the Lexile measure and Lexile scale to match reader with text.

The Lexile Framework provides a common, developmental scale for matching reading ability and text difficulty. Lexile measures enable educators, parents and students to select targeted materials that can improve reading skills and to monitor reading growth across the curriculum, in the library and at home.

Recognized as the most widely adopted reading measure, Lexile measures are used at the school level in various capacities in all 50 states and abroad. Each year, more than 28 million Lexile measures are reported from state and national assessments, classroom assessments and reading programs, representing about half of U.S. students. More than 115,000 books, 80 million articles and 60,000 Web sites have Lexile measures, and these numbers continue to grow.

Attack of the Chicken Nugget Man:
A North Carolina EOG Adventure

520L

ATTACK OF THE CHICKEN NUGGET MAN

A NORTH CAROLINA EOG ADVENTURE

By Kumar Sathy

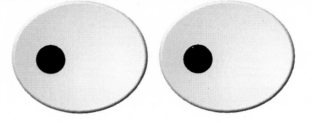

Teaching Standards through Story

A subject-integrated strategic reader aligned with the third grade North Carolina Standard Course of Study for language arts, math, science, and social studies

A STUDENT SOLUTIONS EDUCATIONAL PUBLICATION

Attack of the chicken nugget man: a north carolina eog adventure
ISBN 978-0-9821729-0-2
Library of Congress Control Number: 2008912237
Published by Student Solutions, Inc.
PO Box 2428
Chapel Hill, NC 27515-2428
United States of America
www.student-solutions.org
cnm@student-solutions.org
PATENT PENDING

First Edition | Grade 3 | North Carolina Standard Course of Study
Illustrations by Franfou Studio | Knowledge Nugget Artwork by Christopher Grebb | Clip Art by Nicholas Harrell
This book was created to integrate subjects into a standards-driven reader for third grade students in the state of North Carolina. Versions for other grades and states are currently in development. For information on volume discounts please contact us at cnm@student-solutions.org.

TABLE OF CONTENTS

A Message to Parents

This is a novel (pun intended) children's book. Many editors, educators, and literacy specialists have been consulted to turn this into a valuable (and downright hilarious) resource for families and schools. If you have questions, concerns, and/or praise (we love praise), e-mail us at feedback@chickennuggetman.com. We can't respond to every e-mail, but we read them all.

This is not your standard children's book. It is, however, *driven* by standards. Standards are course concepts approved by a state's board of education and/or public instruction agency. They are the skills and concepts that are taught and tested in schools.

Teachers are experts at executing standards-driven instruction, but standards should not just be taught at school. To help you teach standards at home, you'll see subscripts next to sentences (e.g., M22) in the book. The subscripts correlate to a table of referenced standards at the end of the book. Visit *www.chickennuggetman.com* for updates.

Children aren't going to master standards just by reading this book. The references to standards are, as we call it in education, teachable moments. It is up to teachers and parents to discuss the referenced standards with children and to check for understanding.

Written by an experienced educator, this book was designed to exemplify the principles of instructional best practices, strategic reading, and subject integration. Most books take on the "read first, ask questions later" mentality...literally! Comprehension questions don't create strategic readers. Strategic reading creates strategic readers. Comprehension questions are just one component of active reading. The comprehension questions in this book are primarily higher order questions that are often used in high stakes tests and ask more than "Who is the main character?" They require kids to think critically.

The fact is, many kids don't know how to engage in active, strategic reading. They need constant reminders to empathize with characters, check for understanding, and reread when necessary. Such reminders are embedded in this story to help kids self-monitor and avoid passive reading. The book doesn't use a lecturing tone. It weaves subtle curriculum references and goofy humor into a fictional storyline that makes learning fun.

It is important to understand that this is not a book about kids with perfect behavior. Some characters are silly, a few are bullies, and one even has a tendency to stick things up his nose. The narrator explains, in a kid-friendly tone, why poor behavioral choices are problematic and prompts students to suggest more responsible replacement behaviors. The main character is a model of student resilience. The book equips students with the tools necessary to bounce back from adversity. We encourage you to read it yourself to ensure that it is up to *your* standards.

A MESSAGE TO EDUCATORS

We know your plight. You have to prepare your students to pass high stakes tests using fundamentally flawed resources. Textbooks teach standards but won't necessarily win any awards for student engagement or readability. Fiction books found in bookstores are often highly engaging but don't teach standards or course concepts that are tested at the end of the year, and finding engaging fiction books that are written at an early third grade level can be tricky. Nonfiction guided reading books are full of fun pictures and tend to teach broader standards, but it's hard to find any that teach the specific concepts addressed in the standard course of study. Let's face it, you don't often find these nonfiction books glued to the foreheads of reluctant readers (unless you haven't spelled out the ground rules for glue usage in your classroom). You have to figure out how to teach hundreds of standards, find books that match your students' reading levels, and find instructional materials that even reluctant readers will find interesting. Well, it's all in your hands...literally.

Compare our Lexile® reader measure to the reading levels of your students. This book is perfect for third graders. Why isn't it written on a higher level? It's created for comprehension. We didn't want text complexity to interrupt the strategic reading process.

You'll love the features in this book. It has the instructional qualities of textbooks; the readability, humor, and engagement of bookstore fiction; the literature study qualities of guided reading texts; and the intuitive qualities of experienced teachers. Yes, the book actually reminds students to engage in strategic reading. It calls on students to recall plot components and suggests that they go back and reread when they can't remember such details. It poses higher order comprehension questions based on Bloom's Taxonomy and NC Thinking Skills. There are labeled pictures embedded in the text to help English Language Learners and struggling readers with tricky words. Readers are constantly asked to draw upon prior knowledge before reading on. Finally, they are exposed to 100% of the tested standards for language arts, math, science, and social studies through a silly fictional plot.

You can use this book as a guided reader, independent reader, read-aloud, or literature study/circle. If you use it as a read-aloud, just change the language when you read aloud the contents of the black boxes on the pages. Those boxes tend to say things like "As you read." You can change it to "As we read." The standards table at the end lists the course concepts referenced on each page for you to use as a segue to a lesson on that concept. The references to standards in the text are often subtle and are meant to serve as teachable moments, not as substitutes for rigorous instruction. We know you'll enjoy it!

Beware: What may appear to be a normal, harmless chicken nugget -- just your standard deep-fried chicken product -- may in fact be much, much more.

BURPING PURPLE PRINCIPALS

Lizard

In Chris Robb's dream, his principal was a three-legged, purple <u>lizard</u> who burped up teachers. A horn woke Chris up. It scared the crackers out of him. He fell right out of the

Hamster

bed, landing face-first in the dog's water dish. His sister must have put it there so Chris would step in it. All Chris was wearing when he got up were his Happy <u>Hamster</u> boxer

Mustache

shorts. Well, that and a dog water <u>mustache</u>. And yes, he had a morning <u>wedgie</u>.

Wedgie

Chris was in a rush. The school bus was about to leave. He was in such a hurry that he put on his sister's pink socks by accident. As he ran to the bus, papers flew out of his

Toothbrush

book bag. His <u>toothbrush</u> was still in his mouth. He looked like a crazy kid who forgot to pack his brain.

You'll see notes like this while you read. They'll help you understand the story. STOP and read them. Don't worry about the tiny letters/numbers next to them (like the E9 at the end of this one). E9

Blindfolded Baboon

Chris got on the bus. The driver just stared at him. It looked like Chris had been dressed by a blindfolded baboon.

Chris felt strange. It felt like he forgot something. He just couldn't put his toothpaste-covered finger on it.

Make a prediction. That means to make a smart guess about what might happen next. Do you think Chris will find out he's wearing his sister's socks before he gets off the bus? E8, E4

Chris looked down to make sure he was wearing pants. It wouldn't be the first time he forgot to put on pants. The good news is that he had on pants. After all, Chris really didn't feel like showing the whole school his Happy Hamster boxer shorts. And trust me, the whole school didn't want to see them. The bad news is that he had no idea he was wearing his sister's pink socks.

Chris found a seat near the back of the bus. He looked at the window. It had an alarm button. He was supposed to press it if he saw the Chicken Nugget Man.

Why do you think there's a Chicken Nugget Man alarm on the bus? E8

For the love of sweaty bacon soda, answer these questions!

Analysis Question
If Chris hadn't woken up so late, what events in the story would be different? [E8]

Synthesis Question
What do you think happens when someone presses a Chicken Nugget Man alarm button? [E8, E11, E15]

Evaluation Question
What would you do if you kept waking up late every day? How would you make sure you wouldn't make the same mistakes as Chris? [E8, E15]

RIGHT DOWN THE TOILET! 2

Think about what you've already learned about Chris. If you don't remember very much, go back and reread like adults do when they forget stuff that happens in a story. E7, E8

Okay, you know Chris was in a rush to get to school. You also know he put on his sister's socks by accident. But there's something you don't know about Chris. He gets blamed for everything. Do you know how that feels?[E15,E8,E17] Perhaps a flashback will help.

Toilet

A flashback is like a memory. It's when the author takes you back in time to something that happened earlier. Don't get lost! Just remember that the flashback will end soon! [E4]

A few weeks ago, the <u>toilet</u> in Chris's house broke. His dad figured out the problem.

"Why'd you do this?" Chris's dad yelled. His face puffed up.

Explode

Beet

Wrinkle

It looked like an <u>exploding</u> <u>beet</u>. Chris's dad held a soggy cell phone in his hand. It smelled like old cheese. The kind you would find stuck between a grandpa's toes.

"Do what?" Chris asked. Chris stared at the <u>wrinkled</u> phone.

"Chris, you flushed your sister's cell phone down the toilet!" Chris's dad yelled.

Chris's dad was wrong. Chris didn't do it. But he also didn't try to defend himself.

So how did it happen? Who's to blame?[E7] Chris's sister. She got mad at some boy who called her. She was

KNOWLEDGE NUGGET
SS24
SS26

Cell phones are one type of technology that has changed the way people around the world do business. Now, people can send pictures and emails from anywhere on cell phones.

mad enough that she threw her own phone into the toilet and flushed it. That's what happens when people take their anger out on things. She should have just taken a deep breath to calm down. Instead, the cell phone took a deep dive into the toilet water.

Why didn't Chris try to defend himself? In other words, why didn't he try to explain that it wasn't his fault? E4, E8, E10, E11, E15

Chris still got blamed. He always got blamed. It happened at home. It happened at school. It happened on the bus. This morning, it happened while he was asleep on the bus.

The flashback's over. We're back on the bus with Chris. Try to remember the last thing that happened on the bus. If you don't remember much, just reread! E6, E7, E8

Chris couldn't stand the bus. On a good day, it smelled like a skunk festival. On a bad day, it smelled like, well—I probably shouldn't say because then this book would be rated R and your teacher would chase after me with a frying pan. Trust me.

Anyway, the smell wasn't the worst part. It was the bumpy ride. Every day after he got off the bus, Chris had a headache and his bottom hurt for at least thirty minutes. How could he make the smelly, bumpy bus ride any better? There was only one answer. Chris closed his eyes and fell asleep. He went back to his dream about the burping purple principal.

Can you remember any more details (information) about Chris's dream from the beginning of the story? If not, go back and reread. Good readers reread when they forget details. [E8]

So, what do you think Chris got blamed for on the bus that morning?[E8] Nothing big. Just the craziest bus ride in school history! It all started with Preston. Preston was in Chris's class. He was about to make Chris's morning even worse.

Smiling

Yes, this would go down as one of the saddest mornings in Chris's life. By the time it was over, the only thing happy about Chris was the <u>smiling</u> hamster on his underpants.

For the love of sweaty bacon soda, answer these questions!

<u>Analysis Question</u>
What do you think would have happened if Chris had told his dad that he wasn't the one who flushed the phone down the toilet? E8, E15, E16

<u>Synthesis Question</u>
Can you design a cell phone that won't let you flush it down the toilet? How would it stop you from flushing it? E15

<u>Evaluation Question</u>
What would have been a better way for Chris's dad to find out who flushed the phone down the toilet? E8, E11, E15, E16

WHAT A CRAZY BUS RIDE!

The chapter title tells you that the setting is going to be the bus. Before you read, think about what you already know about the bus. This will help you understand the chapter. [E7]

Preston sat at the back of the bus. He had a little problem. He was thirsty. He could have just waited until he got to school to get some water. But Preston liked to start trouble. So what

Thermos

do you think he did?[E8, E15]

Kindergartener

Preston stole a <u>kindergartener's</u> yellow *Captain Stinkypants* <u>Thermos</u> and drank from it. Katie, the kindergartener, was busy licking a <u>lollipop</u> when Preston grabbed the Thermos right out of her hand. Katie cried her eyes out. She cried so loud that the girl in the seat behind her cried, too! Soon all the kindergarteners on the bus were crying. It was raining

Lollipop

tears and snot. What a mess! Preston should have known better.

Pencil Shavings

There was something Preston didn't know about that Thermos. Katie didn't use it for drinks. It did have some old, spoiled juice in it, but only because Katie never cleaned it. She used the Thermos to hold <u>pencil shavings</u>. In fact, it had three weeks worth of pencil shavings inside. Just multiply the number of weeks times the number of days in a week (3 x 7). That's twenty-one *days* worth of pencil shavings.[M3] That's enough pencil shavings to fill an elephant's underwear.

Preston poured about half a cup of the pencil-flavored juice into his mouth.[M5]

Tongue

He made a horrible face. It looked like he was chewing on bones. Once his greedy little <u>tongue</u> got a

KNOWLEDGE NUGGET

S20

Bones are very important. They protect organs like your heart. Your spine has lots of tiny bones so you can be flexible and bend. They probably don't taste very good, though.

taste of the pencil shaving smoothie, he spat it out like a sprinkler. It landed all over some big kid's head. But it wasn't just any big kid. It was Bobby Rough.

Bobby was the school bully. He was busy yelling at a second-grader when Preston spat all over his face. A few pencil shavings landed in Bobby's mouth.

See if you can sequence (put in order) what just happened. Preston stole a Thermos. What happened next? Then what happened to Bobby? E4, E8, E10

Glue

Guess what happened next? It was crazy! Well, Katie cried even louder. She cried as if someone had glued two onions to her eyes. Bobby punched the seat in front of him. This made the girl sitting

Bubblegum

there spit out her bubblegum. It landed in some boy's ear. Bobby then shook his head from side to side like a big wet dog. He slapped his hands against his face over and over to get the shavings off of his face. Then he started growling. But it didn't end there.

Bobby scratched his tongue with his fingers. He had to get the taste of the pencil shavings out of his mouth. It didn't work. The shavings tasted gross but his dirty yellow nails were worse! You won't believe what he did next. He started rubbing his tongue against the seat. Yes, Bobby Rough, the school bully, was licking the bus seat. Nobody made fun of him though. They were too scared.

Donut

It was sad. If people would just try to be nice to Bobby, they'd see that he wasn't so bad. He looked all big and scary, but he was really as soft as a jelly <u>donut</u>. He even slept with a stuffed pony at night.

It was only when people acted like he was a bully that he actually became a bully. It just goes to show that you can't judge someone just by the way he looks.

Anyway, Bobby didn't know that the nasty stuff in his mouth was actually pencil shavings. All he knew was that it was gross. It was almost as bad as the time his mom made him eat fish waffles.

"What was that stuff?" Bobby yelled.

Scrambled Eggs
and Toast

"Ummm, <u>scrambled eggs and toast</u>?" Preston said, trying to make up a lie. "The bumps in the road made me spit up my breakfast."

"It didn't taste like scrambled eggs and toast!" Bobby yelled.

Katie looked up at Bobby.

"It wasn't scrambled eggs and toast," she cried. "It was pencil shavings from my Thermos."

Bobby turned to Preston. "You eat pencils?" he asked.

Preston tried to think of an excuse. "My doctor told me I need more fiber in my diet." He shouldn't have lied. It just made things worse. Bobby didn't believe him. Now he was angry that Preston lied to him. You see, once you tell one lie, you have to make up another lie to cover that one. It never ends. It's just not worth it.

Preston yelled, "Help!" He knew Bobby was about to do something. The bus driver slammed on the brakes. He parked the bus in the middle of the road. They were stopped in front of Freddie's Fish Shack. The bus driver got up and took a deep breath. You won't believe what he did next. He took off his nasty, stinky, muddy right shoe and waved it around. Everybody covered their noses. The little kids cried. Some of the big kids cried, too!

"Settle down!" the bus driver yelled. "I can't drive with all this noise."

Two nasty smells now filled the air on the bus. The driver's nasty shoe smelled like 34-year-old milk. The fish store made the bus smell like the inside of a trash can. The main idea here is that the bus smelled really bad.[E10, E12]

Do you remember Katie?[E8, E17] Well, the bus smelled so bad that she <u>fainted</u>. She fell flat on the floor. That's when Bobby stole her lollipop. He was still trying to get the taste of pencil shavings out of his mouth. He was also just being a big bully. Bobby

Faint

was the only kid mean enough to take candy from a kindergartener.

Some kid spelled a word wrong on the seat in the last picture. How would you teach that kid the difference between CH and CK? How would you teach him or her to stop writing on seats? E35, SS5

KNOWLEDGE NUGGET

E4

Narrowed is a way of saying "got really small." When people are angry, their eyes narrow. They squint.

Katie woke up. She crawled to her seat. That's when she saw Bobby eating her lollipop. It was just about all her tiny little heart could take. That little girl roared like a tiger. Her eyes <u>narrowed</u>. She bent down. Her bottom waved from side to side. The bus fell silent.

"Nobody takes my lolly," Katie cried. She then hopped over her seat. In mid-air, she grabbed the bus driver's shoe right out of his hand. Arms spread out, she landed on Bobby's back. Sitting on his shoulders, Katie stuck that nasty, smelly shoe right on Bobby's nose. Bobby waved his arms around like an angry ape who had washed his face with hot sauce. The fumes went straight to his brain. He didn't think he was going to make it off the bus alive.

The rest of the kids stared in shock while little Katie went Kung Fu all over Bobby Rough. It looked as if there was a new bully in town.

"Take it away," Bobby cried. "I want my mommy!" He couldn't stand the smell of the shoe any longer. He threw the lollipop back to Katie. By then, it was broken and smelled like dirty mop water. Pieces of it stuck to her <u>sweater</u>.

Sweater

The bus driver grabbed his shoe. He yelled at three kids. Guess who?[E8] He yelled at Katie, Bobby, and Chris. Not Preston though. He always found a way to get out of trouble.

What are some other ways Katie could have gotten her lollipop back without it breaking? [SS5]

Think about who got in trouble. Was it fair?[E11, E15] Chris got blamed for the whole thing, even though he'd been asleep.

Chris didn't try to defend himself. He had given up trying to defend himself when he got blamed for things. He had given up trying to do well in school. He had even given up trying to make friends. The main idea is that Chris had given up trying to do anything.[E7, E10, E12]

For the love of sweaty bacon soda, answer these questions!

Analysis Question
If Preston hadn't taken Katie's Thermos, how would the bus ride have been different? [E15, E16]

Synthesis Question
Can you come up with a creative way for the bus driver to get the kids to settle down that doesn't involve a stinky shoe? [E15]

Evaluation Question
What would have been a better way for Bobby to get the taste of pencil shavings out of his mouth? [E15]

4 NO CHICKEN NUGGETS ALLOWED

> Good readers make predictions. Make a prediction (a smart guess about what might happen next). Do you think anyone will make fun of Chris's socks? E8, E4, E15

The bus finally parked in front of the school. It seemed like the longest ride ever. It would have seemed even longer if the bus driver had taken off both shoes. But then he would have passed out, too! Trust me. It should be against the law to take off those shoes.

At school there were green signs everywhere that read "No Chicken Nuggets Allowed." The signs had been there ever since the Chicken Nugget Man started eating children.

Chicken nuggets were banned. That means nobody was allowed to have them.E4 It wasn't safe. People were scared that the Chicken Nugget Man would hide behind other chicken nuggets. They didn't want him sneaking into the school to eat children. That's why all chicken nuggets were banned.

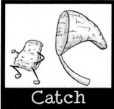
Catch

Nobody knew much about the Chicken Nugget Man. Only kids had ever seen him, but everyone wanted to <u>catch</u> him. He was wanted fried or alive.

Guards stood everywhere. There was a line to get into the building. It was because of the slow Nugget Detectors.

Nugget Detectors were machines.[E4] They were made in

Machine

the Research Triangle Park (RTP) in North Carolina. The detectors tried to catch kids sneaking chicken nuggets into school. There was a <u>scarcity</u> of Nugget Detectors. A lot of people wanted them, but not

KNOWLEDGE NUGGET

SS18

Scarcity also happens to things like crops when there is no rain. No rain means less crops. People still want to buy crops, but they are scarce, so the price goes up.

enough were made. [E4,SS17]

It took a long time to walk through the Nugget Detectors. There were too many kids and not enough guards or Nugget Detectors.

Explain what a Nugget Detector is in your own words. If you can't, just go back and reread. [E12]

Guard

"Son!" a guard yelled at Chris. He was part of a group called the Anti-Chicken Nugget Task Force. They protected kids from the Chicken Nugget Man. "Did you have your book bag on your back all morning? Did anyone try to put anything in it?"

KNOWLEDGE NUGGET

SS22

Some cities need RTP for Nugget Detectors. RTP needs other communities for other things. When communities depend on each other, it's called interdependence.

The prefix "anti" means against. Can you figure out what Anti-Chicken Nugget means? [E1, E2]

Chris answered the guard's questions and moved on.

"Take off your shoes," another guard said, "and put them in the tray."

It normally wasn't a big deal for Chris to take off his shoes. But it was a big deal that day.

Bobby Rough happened to be right behind Chris in line. Remember Bobby? Do you remember what he did to Kung Fu Katie on the bus?[E11] Bobby was mean to everyone. But he was really mean to Chris.

Anyway, Chris took off his shoes. Bobby pointed at Chris's socks and laughed.

"Hey Christina, nice socks!" Bobby yelled.

KNOWLEDGE NUGGET

SS23
SS25
SS27

Governor Luther Hodges helped set up RTP to bring technology jobs to the state. RTP companies research ways to improve technology for us. Hodges was a community leader in technology.

It might sound crazy, but Chris was more scared of Bobby than the Chicken Nugget Man. Yes, the Chicken Nugget Man could swallow Chris in one gulp. Then Chris would have to live inside the Chicken Nugget Man's <u>tummy</u> for the rest of his life. Sure, it would be a little sticky and slimy. It would smell as bad as a <u>sweaty armpit</u>. But it was still better than having Bobby make fun of him in front of the girls in his class.

Sweaty Armpit

Tummy

Chris looked down at his socks. He wanted to see why Bobby had called him a girl's name. He couldn't believe his eyes.

"I'm wearing my sister's socks!" he thought. "Why do they have to be pink? Why do they have to say, 'Girls Rule' in purple glitter?" This really wasn't his day. Even if girls did rule, Chris didn't feel like telling the world about it on a pair of pink socks. Do you remember why he was wearing pink socks?[E7, E10] If you're a good reader, you know that Chris put on his sister's socks by accident. It was because he got dressed in a hurry that morning.

Anyway, the guard wouldn't let Chris take off the socks. Chris had to figure out how to get rid of them. If not, he'd have to hear Bobby's big, fat, donut-chewing, <u>pretzel</u>-eating, ice-cream-licking mouth running all day long about those pink socks.

Pretzel

KNOWLEDGE NUGGET

M13

Let's do a little math problem. Probability is another way of stating the chance that something will happen. If the probability of Bobby making fun of Chris whenever he sees him is 1 : 2, that means he will tease Chris once every two times that he sees him. Now try to figure out how many times Bobby will tease Chris if he sees him ten times.

For the love of sweaty bacon soda, answer these questions!

Analysis Question
What do you think would have happened if the Chicken Nugget Detector had actually detected a chicken nugget in Chris's pocket? E8, E15, E16

Synthesis Question
Can you design a better Chicken Nugget Detector that wouldn't cause such long lines? How would it work faster than the one in the book? E15

Evaluation Question
Do you agree with Chris? Would you be more scared of Bobby Rough than the Chicken Nugget Man? E8, E15, E16

A STRAWBERRY MILK MUSTACHE

Make a prediction. How will Chris try to get rid of the socks? [E8, E4, E15]

Restroom

The bell rang. It was too late to go to the <u>restroom</u> to take off the socks. Chris looked for an empty corner. The principal saw him.

"Chris Robb!" Mr. Turner yelled. "Where are your shoes?"

Chris was normally scared of Mr. Turner. Today

Strawberry

was different. Mr. Turner had <u>strawberry</u> milk all over his face. It dripped from his chin. Chris smiled. He couldn't help it. He should have at least tried not to smile.

"Son, what are you smiling about?" Mr. Turner yelled in a deep voice. "It's not safe to be alone in the hallways. It's also a good way to get in trouble. Do you think it's funny to get in trouble?"

Make another prediction. Do you think Mr. Turner is going to send Chris to the office? What do you think Chris could do to show respect to the principal? E8, E15, E17

"No, sir," Chris said. He knew it was important to respect adults.

The pink milk was now dripping onto Mr. Turner's shirt. Chris couldn't keep a straight face. He needed to do something. He thought about plucking out a nose hair. The pain would make him stop smiling. He should have tried harder to keep a straight face. But trying hard just wasn't something Chris did well.

"Still think it's funny?" Mr. Turner asked. "Don't you know who hides in the halls? The Chicken Nugget Man hides in the halls. He swallows little kids when they're all alone and nobody is there to help them. Think that's funny, Chris?"

As Mr. Turner spoke, pink milk dripped from his mouth. A few drops fell on Chris's socks.

"The only hall you are allowed to be alone in is the one by your classroom. This one isn't safe. And this little corner you're hiding in really isn't safe," Mr. Turner said, spitting milk onto Chris's forehead like

Knee

raindrops of rage. "The Chicken Nugget Man could eat so much of you that your skeleton would be the only thing left of your body.[S19] He would eat your <u>knees</u>,

Sandwich

too. He would use them to make grilled knees <u>sandwiches</u>. One day, you're just a third grader. The next day, you're a bacon, legs, and knees sandwich. Do you really think that's funny, Chris?"

Mountain

Chris was ready to explode with laughter. He was ready to laugh so loud that everyone in the coastal plains of eastern <u>North Carolina</u> and all the way to the

North Carolina

<u>mountains</u> in the western part of the state would hear it.[SS15] That's more than 154 miles![M8] Just look on a map. It's far!

Look at the number 154 on this page. How many different numbers can you make using the numbers 1, 5, and 4? Just mix the numbers up to make new numbers (like 145).[M12]

"Put your shoes on, Chris!" Mr. Turner yelled. "And get to class before I call your parents!" Mr. Turner's white shirt was no longer white. It was now about as pink as Chris's socks. It was a good thing Mr. Turner finally stopped dripping milk onto the floor. If the puddle got any bigger, the kids would have to swim through it to get to class.

"Yes, sir," Chris said quietly. He was still wearing those ugly socks. They were now covered with pink slime. Chris put on his shoes. He always did whatever Mr. Turner asked him to do.

Chris thought about his socks. He needed a better plan. He had to get rid of them before the whole school found out. If anyone else saw his pink socks, even the kids in the *We're Scared of Bunny Rabbits Club* would tease him.

Chris walked to his classroom. Guess who showed up in the hall?[E8, E15] Bobby Rough. Right behind him. Chris's legs shook. The hallway was empty except for Chris, Bobby, the puddle of pink milk, and a splash of grown-up drool.

> Think about what you know about Bobby Rough. Now, predict what he is going to do to Chris. [E8, E10, E15]

Bobby leaned down. He put his hands on his knees like a football player. With a snort like a bull and a grunt like a bear, Bobby charged at Chris. Chris thought this was the end. He pictured his funeral. He imagined how his mom would probably give away all of his video games. Chris moved out of the way. Just in time, too. Bobby was moving *fast*.

Bobby's feet hit the puddle of pink milk. He fell flat on his bottom and slid down the hallway like a bowling ball. But there were no pins waiting for him at the end of the hall. Instead, there was a trashcan. He bumped right into it. Everything inside spilled on top of him. The trashcan was filled with, you guessed it, pencil

Cupcake

shavings. Bobby looked like an angry bully <u>cupcake</u> with brown and gray sprinkles on top.

Do you understand what you just read? Good readers reread what they don't understand. [E7]

For the love of sweaty bacon soda, answer these questions!

Analysis Question
Compare Mr. Turner to Chris's dad. Are they alike in any way? Do they each treat Chris the same way? If you don't remember anything about Chris's dad, go back and reread the chapter about the soggy cell phone. E11, E15, E16

Synthesis Question
What is a crazy way that Chris could have stayed dry when Mr. Turner was spitting milk all over him? E15

Evaluation Question
Can you think of a better way for Chris to stop himself from laughing while talking to Mr. Turner? E15, E17

Chris's teacher had a really silly name. He had never heard of a name so silly. Her name was Ms. Bubblebrain. Chris always seemed to forget how to say it right. One time, he even called her Ms. Bubblegum.

Ms. Bubblebrain didn't mind. There were a few things she understood about Chris. She knew he wasn't making fun of her. She knew he showed respect to her. She knew that Chris always did whatever she asked him to do. She also knew that he had trouble remembering anything he learned in school, even his teacher's name.

Cricket

Her name wasn't the only silly thing about Ms. Bubblebrain. She also shouted the names of really gross foods when she was mad. Ms. Bubblebrain would yell things like hairy <u>cricket</u> <u>biscuits</u> and soggy <u>salmon</u> salami.

Biscuits

Salmon

Chris stood outside of his classroom. That's when he came up with a way to get rid of those ugly socks. It wasn't hard. That was a good thing, because Chris didn't know how to try hard at anything. All he did was look at Smelly Sam's name on the class list posted on the door. The plan just came to him.

Always pay close attention when the author tells you about a new character. [E7]

Smelly Sam was a student in Chris's class. He sat at the back table. You know how kids all do different things when they're bored? Think about what you do.[E17] Some kids chew on pencils. Some tap on desks. Some sit there wishing they lived in a world where they could put their parents in time-out. Others wish they could send their teachers to the principal's office. But what does Smelly Sam do?[E8] He sticks things up his nose until they get stuck.

But he isn't just bored. Smelly Sam had a hard time smelling things. Something was wrong with his nose. That's why he always stuck things up there. It was the only way he knew how things smelled.

KNOWLEDGE NUGGET
S13

Light moves in a straight line until it hits an object (like Smelly Sam's nose) and is reflected and/or absorbed.

Well, that and the fact that Bobby Rough once told him that if he stuck things far enough up his nose, they would end up in China. Nobody knew if Smelly Sam actually believed that.

People didn't really talk to Smelly Sam. They were afraid he'd try

Flashlight

to stuff them up his nose, too. Anyway, whenever Sam

Tweezers

stuffed things up there, Ms. Bubblebrain always saved the day with her <u>tweezers</u>. Once she used a <u>flashlight</u> and a pair of <u>chopsticks</u>.

Here's a little flashback about the chopsticks. It will

Chopsticks

help you understand how Sam got the name Smelly Sam. It happened after a field trip to a <u>Japanese</u> <u>restaurant</u>.

Japanese Restaurant

Something smelled bad on the bus. Everybody opened their windows. But the smell wouldn't leave. It all started at the restaurant when Smelly Sam wanted to know what fish smelled like. He snuck a piece of fish into his pocket and got on the bus. Think about what you already know about Smelly Sam. What do you think he did next?[E8, E15]

Yes, he stuck a piece of fish up his nose. Ms. Bubblebrain didn't have her tweezers. All she had were chopsticks from the restaurant. Ms. Bubblebrain slowly pulled the slimy piece of fish out of Sam's nose.

Strong

After that day, Sam was known as Smelly Sam.

He didn't mind being called Smelly Sam. Think about it. Any kid who sticks things up his nose at school and lives to talk about it has to be pretty <u>strong</u>.

Can you name a kid in this story who isn't as strong as Smelly Sam? Is there a kid who isn't as strong as Smelly Sam when people call him names? [E8, E11, E15, E16]

Now you know about Smelly Sam. It's time to get back to our main character. At this point in the story, Chris is outside of Ms. Bubblebrain's classroom. He just got in trouble for being in the hall.

Well, Chris had finally come up with a plan that had something to do with Smelly Sam. And it was about to cause one giant mess.

Can you figure out Chris's new plan? Think about what you know about Smelly Sam. If you don't remember very much, go back and reread this chapter. E7, E8, E15

For the love of sweaty bacon soda, answer these questions!

Analysis Question
How is the way Chris treats Ms. Bubblebrain similar to the way he treats Mr. Turner? E8, E11, E16

Synthesis Question
Can you design a crazy device (like a machine or other object) that will stop Smelly Sam from sticking things up his nose? How would it work? E15

Evaluation Question
Are you as strong as Smelly Sam is? If someone called you smelly or made fun of you in some other way, would it bother you? E8, E11, E15

CHRIS JUST DOESN'T TRY

Think about what you already know about Ms. Bubblebrain. What do you think she'll do when Chris walks in late? E8, E15

Chris opened the door. Ms. Bubblebrain looked up. She was angry. She yelled so loud that half of the class (that's the same as 2/4 or even 10/20 of the class) got scared.M5

"Sweet chalk-filled chicken!" Ms. Bubblebrain screamed. "Chris! You're late again!"

"Sorry, Ms. Bobblehead," Chris said.

"It's Ms. Bubblebrain! Chris, you need to try harder to remember things," Ms. Bubblebrain said.

"Sorry, ma'am," Chris said. The truth is that Chris didn't know how to try harder. He couldn't remember ever trying hard to do anything!

Ms. Bubblebrain knew Chris was forgetful. She thought he would forget to wear his own eyeballs to school if they weren't already stuck in his head.

The rest of the class just laughed.

Chris is polite to his teacher. It's too bad he can't remember her name. Can you remember what other adult in the story he was polite to? Go back and find out what page it was on. E7, E8, E11

"Go join Tommy," Ms. Bubblebrain said. "You're working with him today. We're learning about maps."

"Why do I have to work with Tuna Tommy?" Chris thought. He didn't say it out loud. That would just be mean.

No one liked working with Tuna Tommy. He stuffed food in his desk as if it were his own personal fridge. He would leave food there and forget about it for weeks. Sometimes he left the rotting food in his desk for months. Sometimes armies of ants ate the rotting food. And once, the rotting food grew a green, sweaty, moldy wig! But I'll tell you more about that later.

Tommy was his real name. Everyone called him Tuna Tommy. It's because his teacher found rotten tuna salad in his desk way back in the first grade. Tuna Tommy didn't mind the name. His parents raised him to be strong. He didn't care what other kids called him.

Chris really didn't want to work with Tuna Tommy. Who knew what was in his desk that day? There could be mutant flies with gorilla arms feeding on the rotten food inside!

"Can I use the restroom?" Chris asked. He didn't need to go. He just wanted to get rid of his socks.

Bicep

"Why in the name of peanut butter and <u>bicep</u> sandwiches do you need to go to the restroom? It's only ten minutes to nine!" Ms. Bubblebrain said. [M7]

Chris looked clueless.

Okay, you know what "clue" means. The suffix "less" means less of or without. Now, can you figure out what "clueless" means? [E1, E2]

"He doesn't even know what a bicep is!" someone yelled.

"Chris, do you know what a bicep is?" Ms. Bubblebrain asked.

Chris dropped his head. "No, ma'am," he said.

"We learned that yesterday," Ms. Bubblebrain said. "You need to pay attention in class. Biceps are muscles. They're on top of your arms. They help you lift and pull things." S22, S23

Chris didn't get it. He always mixed up biceps with triceps.

"Just go join Tommy," Ms. Bubblebrain said. "Try to learn something about maps. If you do, I'll let you go to the restroom. Tell me how to find Burlington, North Carolina, on a map," Ms. Bubblebrain said.

Ms. Bubblebrain had given him a chance to go to the restroom. Chris forgot the plan he had come up with in the hall. If he could just explain how to find Burlington, she would let him go! He'd be able to flush those socks down the toilet. Then he wouldn't be the one wearing pink socks. A <u>sewer</u> rat would be wearing them.

Sewer

If you can't remember Chris's plan involving Smelly Sam, don't worry. I haven't told you his plan yet. Try to guess what it is and keep reading! You're doing great! E8

For the love of sweaty bacon soda, answer these questions!
Analysis Question
How is Tuna Tommy similar to Smelly Sam? E8, E15, E16
Synthesis Question
Can you design something that would stop Tuna Tommy from stuffing food in his desk? How would it work? E15
Evaluation Question
Can you think of a better way for Ms. Bubblebrain to talk to Chris at the beginning of the chapter so that the class wouldn't laugh at him? E8, E15

Raspberry Meat loaf

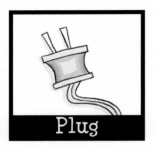

Plug

Chris <u>plugged</u> his nose because Tuna Tommy's desk smelled so bad. He asked Tommy a question about maps.

Chris's plugged nose made his words sound weird. Tuna Tommy couldn't understand him. Chris tried again.

"Tommy, I need to find a city on a map."

"What?" Tommy asked.

Chris had to make a decision. If he unplugged his nose, he'd smell the rotten food in Tuna Tommy's desk. If he didn't, Tommy wouldn't be able to understand him, and he'd never earn that trip to the restroom. He decided that smelling rotten food was better than being teased about pink socks. Chris unplugged his nose.

"I need to find a city on a map," Chris said.

"Oh," Tuna Tommy said. "What city?"

Chris didn't even try to remember. He guessed.

"I think it's America," Chris said.

"That's not a city," Tommy said. "It's a country."

North America

"Fine," Chris said. "North America."

"That's not a city, it's a continent."

Chris remembered the city started with a "B."

"Billy Goat!" he yelled.

"That's a farm animal. Chris, do you mean Burlington?"

"Yeah, that one!" Chris said.

Tuna Tommy couldn't figure out how Chris had made it past preschool.

Compass

"Are you trying to find out what Burlington is near? Or exactly where it is?" Tommy asked.

Tommy could tell that Chris had no idea what he was talking about.

"Look," Tommy said, "you use a compass rose to find out what a city is close to. Use grids to see exactly where it is. Grids are lines. They help you find things. In this case, a city." [SS14]

"Okay, I think I got it," Chris said.

There was so much to remember. All the words were so big. Chris should have asked a few questions. Asking <u>questions</u> is a good way to make sure you learn things.

Question

Before you read on, see if you're smarter than Chris. Can you remember what Tuna Tommy taught Chris about maps? Don't peek until you've tried to answer it on your own. ^{SS14, E17}

"Compass rose, grids. Rose, grids. Rose grids," Chris said to himself. He walked up to Ms. Bubblebrain.

"Here's a map," Ms. Bubblebrain said. "How do you find a city in North Carolina?"

"Okay," Chris said. "You use this flower called a compass. It shows you what is close to the city. To see exactly where it is, you use grits."

"You use what?" Ms. Bubblebrain asked.

"Grits," Chris said.

"Son!" Ms. Bubblebrain yelled. "What in the name of raspberry meat loaf are you talking about? You can't use grits to find a city! Grits are a breakfast food. All the ice-cream-filled, hot-sauce-covered grits in the world won't help you find a city on a map!"

Bumblebee

"But Ms. <u>Bumblebee</u>, couldn't you just follow the smell of the grits until you found the city?" Chris asked.

"No, son," Ms. Bubblebrain said to Chris. She was starting to think that a family of dancing donkeys was running his brain. "And it's Bubblebrain, not Bumblebee. You're just not trying hard enough, Chris."

Chris smelled his way back to Tuna Tommy's desk. He wished that he wasn't so forgetful. His tummy hurt.

It wasn't just because Ms. Bubblebrain's <u>recipe</u> for grits was gross. His tummy hurt the way it always did when he couldn't remember things. He was tired of people telling him to try harder. If he knew how to try harder, he would.

Recipe

Can you find the footprint that is on the North Carolina map in the picture? What are the coordinates? Your answer should have two numbers, such as (2,1). E19, M10

"How did you just forget what I taught you?" Tuna Tommy asked.

"You heard Ms. Bubblebunny," Chris said. "I don't try hard enough. Just leave me alone."

Chris thought he would never get rid of his socks. He had to think of something. Those socks made him a walking bully magnet.

Was Ms. Bubblebrain being fair when she wouldn't let Chris use the restroom? Was Chris being fair when he told Tuna Tommy to leave him alone? Why or why not? E11, E15

For the love of sweaty bacon soda, answer these questions!

Analysis Question
If Chris had actually remembered what Tuna Tommy taught him, how would this chapter have ended? E8, E15, E16

Synthesis Question
What could Chris have done to make sure he actually learned what Tuna Tommy taught him about maps? E8, E11, E15

Evaluation Question
Are you a forgetful person at school? What do you do when you don't understand something your teacher says? E8, E15, E17

OPERATION SMELLY SAM

Can you remember how Chris has already tried to get rid of the pink socks? [E7, E8]

Okay, it's time for a quick summary.[E10, E12] You already know why Chris is trying to get rid of the socks. Outside of his classroom, he came up with a plan that had to do with Smelly Sam. But then Ms. Bubblebrain gave him a chance to earn a trip to the restroom. This made him forget his plan.

When the map test ended in failure, Chris was about to give up. Then he remembered his Smelly Sam plan. It was perfect. Chris knew Smelly Sam liked smelling things. He also knew that Sam had to put things way up his nose in order to smell them.

"Hey Sam," Chris said. "Come here."

About half a minute (or 30 seconds) later,[M7] Ms. Bubblebrain's face looked like a toilet about to explode.

Can you guess why Ms. Bubblebrain is so angry? Stop for a second and predict what Chris did. [E8]

"Sam!" Ms. Bubblebrain yelled. "Why in the name of hairy rabbit's milk are you stuffing a sock up your nose?"

Ms. Bubblebrain sent Chris to the office. It's a really bad idea to make someone smell socks that have your toe juice all over them.

The principal made Chris put the slimy socks back on his feet. He made him do this even though they had been inside Smelly Sam's nose. The only good thing about this was that Sam's nose made the socks all warm and toasty.

Chris couldn't stand going to the office. But that wasn't the worst part. The worst part was feeling bad for Smelly Sam. The socks smelled so bad that Sam would have that nasty smell stuck in his nose for three days. Poor kid.

On the way back to class, Chris ran into Mr. Wit. He was the Assistant Principal.

"Yo," Mr. Wit said.

Chris almost smiled.

"So I heard, you know, about the sock thing," Mr. Wit said.

Chris lowered his head.

"I did something like that once," Mr. Wit said, fixing his tie. "Back in the fourth grade." Mr. Wit smiled. "Made some kid smell my gym bag. Poor kid ended up

KNOWLEDGE NUGGET

SS19

Mr. Wit is a worker who specializes in leading schools. That means he went to college to learn that special job. Schools divide up work to make things easier. If not, your teacher would work in the library, the cafeteria AND your classroom!

throwing up all over my tennis shoes. Lost a lot of friends. Not to mention a great pair of shoes. But yeah, I really did lose some friends over that one. And not just because I smelled like, well, you know, for the rest of the day. Turns out those other kids were afraid I'd make *them* smell my gym bag, too. It's okay, though. You're a kid. You're allowed to make mistakes. It's my job to make sure you don't keep making them. Just don't let this one ruin your day."

Chris wasn't planning to say anything, but the words poured out of his mouth. It was easy to talk to Mr. Wit.

"Mr. Turner doesn't like me," Chris said. "He made me wear the socks even after --"

"Chris," Mr. Wit interrupted. He leaned on the wall. He wasn't mad. "Do you know for a fact that the principal doesn't like you? Or is that just your opinion?"

Chris didn't answer. He didn't have to. Mr. Wit knew the truth.

"I used to think my principal didn't like me when I was a kid. It's normal. What you don't know is that Mr. Turner has to deal with many kids who act up all day. They lie. They don't show respect. They stop other kids from learning. And they just never admit what they did wrong. Sometimes, that's all he wants to hear. But the kids think he's always going to punish them. If they just gave the guy a chance --"

Mr. Wit didn't finish. He could see that Chris got the main idea. Give people a chance. Chris had figured that Mr. Turner didn't like him. He never gave Mr. Turner a chance. Chris never thought about the things Mr. Turner did to prove that he liked Chris. He only thought about the things Mr. Turner did that seemed to show that he didn't like Chris.

"You're a good kid," Mr. Wit said. "You'll learn. Anyway, it's over now. Shake it off. I don't want you getting into any more trouble. And Chris," he continued.

Chris looked up.

"Try to keep your socks on your feet and out of Sam's nose, okay?" Mr. Wit smiled. He put his hand on Chris's shoulder.

Chris smiled, too. But he quickly covered it up.

Mr. Wit turned around and walked the other way.

"Is that it?" Chris asked. He meant to say it in his head, but he said it out loud.

"I don't have to punish you just to get you to make better choices," Mr. Wit said.

That was the thing about Mr. Wit. He didn't take everything so seriously. Chris wanted to thank him. But for some reason, he didn't.

For the love of sweaty bacon soda, answer these questions!

Analysis Question
Really bad things happened when Chris talked Smelly Sam into sticking socks up his nose. What are some other bad things that could have happened? [E8, E15]

Synthesis Question
If you were Chris, what would you do to get rid of the socks? [E15, E17]

Evaluation Question
How do you feel about the way Chris used Smelly Sam? What should Chris do to make things better? [E8, E15, E17]

BROCCOLI-FILLED CHEESECAKE

It was a few minutes before lunch, and Ms. Bubblebrain was teaching the class about capital letters. She told the kids to use capital letters in names. "The names of places, days, events, and titles all need capital letters,"[E31] she said. She talked for a few more minutes about capital letters. She told the class that names of places like states and continents need capital letters.[E31]

Cockroach

Chris wasn't paying attention to the lesson. He was daydreaming. In his daydream, Ms. Bubblebrain was a <u>cockroach</u>. A big smelly foot was chasing her. Guess what the foot was wearing?[E8] You guessed it, a pink sock. If you're a good reader, you know what words were on it.

Ms. Bubblebrain told the class to line up for lunch. She also told the kids that after lunch, she was going to ask someone to tell her about capital letters.

11:50
Lunch in 10 minutes
Girls rule
Chicken Nuggets Banned by Federal Law
CHICKEN NUGGET ALARM
Pull in case of Chicken Nugget Man sighting
Capitalization Rules: Capitalize the names of things: [E31]
* Places (Proper nouns, continents, countries, states, cities...)
*Days
*Events (historical events, wars, holidays...)
*Titles
ALWAYS CAPITALIZE THE FIRST WORD IN A SENTENCE
Capitalize the names of things

After lunch, Ms. Bubblebrain read a story about the Chicken Nugget Man. It was written by the Anti-Chicken Nugget Task Force. Sometimes, Chris had a hard time believing those stories. The stories taught kids to stay away from the Chicken Nugget Man. Chris's mind wandered off during the story, and before he knew it, it was almost time for recess.

"I almost forgot," Ms. Bubblebrain said. "Someone tell me three things that need capital letters."

Chris tried to hide behind his book. He hoped Ms. Bubblebrain wouldn't call on him. He hadn't paid attention at all. He thought capital letters were giant alphabet people who lived in Raleigh. Poor Chris, he was really going to get teased for this one.

"Chris Robb," Ms. Bubblebrain said.

Chris didn't want to hear her say that he wasn't trying to pay attention. He already knew he wasn't trying. He needed an excuse.

"Can I tell you the answer later?" Chris said. "I can't think about capital letters right now. I can only think about one thing at a time, and right now, I'm thinking about how badly I need to use the restroom."

Thirsty

Chris wasn't lying. He really had to go to the restroom. He had been really <u>thirsty</u> at lunch and drank five milks. That's five half-pints! Drinking 40 ounces of milk would make anyone have to go to the restroom!^M8

Ms. Bubblebrain didn't believe Chris.

"He drank five milks at lunch," Tuna Tommy said. "He isn't lying. He really needs to go." Tuna Tommy was the only kid in the school that was nice to Chris. You'll find out why a little bit later. For now, we need to think about Chris. After all, he REALLY had to go to the restroom.

"Fine," Ms. Bubblebrain said. "Go ahead, but we're going to recess in a few minutes. Be outside seven minutes before 1:42."^M7 That was Ms. Bubblebrain's way of giving Chris a math problem. "And stay in our hall," she added. "It has Nugget Detectors. Nobody knows where the Chicken Nugget Man will attack next. If you're late, I'll send you to the office faster than you can say <u>broccoli</u>-filled cheesecake."

Broccoli

"Yes, ma'am," Chris said. "Thank you for letting

me go." Chris knew it was important to show respect to adults. He learned that the day his dad took away his Internet access because Chris made fun of a sweater his mom made for the dog. The sweater was too small. It made the dog's eyes bulge out of his head.

KNOWLEDGE NUGGET

SS24

Chris uses technology to buy stuff online. Technology has changed the way people do business and has helped a lot of companies and local economies grow.

Sadly, Chris had been planning to use the Internet to print out all the things he wanted his parents to buy for his birthday. Chris's dad gave him a long speech about showing respect. Chris usually forgot this lesson, but sometimes he remembered that showing respect kept him from getting into more trouble.

Chris passed many signs in the hallway. They all said "Chicken Nuggets Banned by Federal Law." There were four signs in each of the three hallways. Chris wondered how many signs there were in all.[M3]

Water Fountain

Chris saw Mr. Turner. He was with Mr. Wit. They were talking about how to keep students safe. Chris heard them say that a crying first-grader thought she saw the Chicken Nugget Man near a <u>water fountain</u> that morning.

Chris shouldn't have been so nosy. He just wanted to know what Mr. Wit had to say. He was the only adult who didn't yell at Chris, and he always gave Chris a chance to explain himself. It seemed like every other adult had <u>labeled</u> Chris as a troublemaker.

Label

Chris couldn't do Ms. Bubblebrain's math problem. Seven minutes before 1:42? He had no idea what time that was. Math was his worst subject. Wait, that's not true. *Every* subject was his worst subject. Chris didn't get good grades. Well, that's not exactly true. He once got an *A+* on a test that had only one question (5 x Z = 35).[M16] He had to figure out what Z was equal to.[M17] It was multiple choice. He guessed, and he got it right.

It's not like he could have cheated off of a friend. Chris didn't have friends. Well, that's not exactly true either. Remember Tuna Tommy? He was nice to Chris. That's because of something that happened at lunch one day. Chris gave Tuna Tommy ¼ of his <u>cheeseburger</u> because he was full after eating the rest.

Cheeseburger

What fraction of the cheeseburger did Chris eat? Hint: It's not ¼. [M5, M6]

Since then, Tuna Tommy has been nice to Chris. It's Tuna Tommy who doesn't have many friends.

For the love of sweaty bacon soda, answer these questions!
Analysis Question
What do you think was going on in Chris's head when Ms. Bubblebrain was about to call on someone to tell her three things about capital letters? [E8, E11, E15]
Synthesis Question
Can you come up with a crazy way to stop Chris from daydreaming? [E15]
Evaluation Question
Ms. Bubblebrain probably could tell that Chris was daydreaming. Do you think it was a good idea or a bad idea for her to call on him to answer a question while he wasn't paying attention? [E15]

TUNA TOMMY

Chris walked back to the classroom. It was as empty as the friends list in Bobby Rough's cell phone. Do you remember where everybody went? The other kids were at recess. If Chris tried to remember where they were, he'd figure it out. But we all know that Chris didn't try very hard to remember things.

Nickel

Chris looked at the fake <u>nickels</u> on the table and guessed that the class was going to have a math lesson on money later. Or maybe Bobby Rough tricked Alex into trading in his lunch money for fake money again, and Alex left it in the room. It happened all the time. Chris always felt bad for Alex when he tried to give the lunch lady fake money.

"Boy!" the lunch lady always said. "I was born at night, but I wasn't born last night! That money is about as fake as the chicken we served on Friday! How many times do I have to tell you to stop giving that boy your lunch money?"

Chris saw a pattern on the table. The first row had 1 nickel in it. The next row had 3 nickels. The last row had 9 nickels. He knew each number was getting bigger, but he had no idea how to find the next number in the pattern.[M14, M15] Was he supposed to multiply? Was he supposed to add?

If you continue the pattern of nickels, how many nickels would be in the fourth row? How much money is that? [M14, M15]

Hairball

Chris heard the water fountain in the hallway. It was shaking. He had a feeling something scary was about to happen. He was right.

The door to the classroom closed on its own. Chris was about to freak out like Carmela had when she found a <u>hairball</u> in her cheeseburger at lunch. But something else caught his attention.

Something in the room smelled bad. It smelled so bad that Chris didn't even think about the door. He could barely breathe. He wanted to find the source of the stink. It was a good thing Kung Fu Katie wasn't there. She would have passed out again!

Chris wasn't a bad kid. He just made bad choices. He decided to stay in the room alone and figure out what smelled.

It wasn't hard to figure it out. It was Tuna Tommy's desk. It smelled like moldy cheese that had been sitting there since the 1600s. Chris decided to find out what was inside Tuna Tommy's desk.

KNOWLEDGE NUGGET
SS10 SS11

In the 1600s, most settlers in NC sold crops for money. Now most people sell very different things because our way of life has changed.

KNOWLEDGE NUGGET
SS8 SS9

In the 1800s, boys were taught to grow up and continue their fathers' jobs. Now, boys can have any job they want!

Be creative: Name the smelliest food that could be rotting inside Tuna Tommy's desk. [E15]

For the love of sweaty bacon soda, answer these questions!

Analysis Question
What would have happened if Ms. Bubblebrain had walked into the room while Chris was standing next to Tuna Tommy's desk? [E8, E15, E16]

Synthesis Question
What is something that could have happened in the story to distract Chris so he wouldn't try to find out what was in Tuna Tommy's desk? [E8, E15]

Evaluation Question
If you were in that room alone, would you be curious enough to want to see what was in that desk, even if you knew you would get in trouble? [E15, E17]

If you could ask the author any question about the story right now, what would you ask? [E8]

Chris really wanted to know what was in that desk. He stuck his hand inside. He felt a packet of BBQ sauce, worksheets, and broken pencils. Chris thought he heard strange noises coming from the desk. He was about to look inside but something else caught his attention.

Chris finally figured out what was stinking up the room. It was a green cupcake. It had fuzzy black <u>frosting</u> on top, and it read "Happy Birthday, Carmela!"

Frosting

If you think that's bad, you need to hear a little more about that smelly cupcake. It wouldn't have smelled so bad if Carmela's birthday had been a few days ago. The thing is that Carmela's birthday had been four months ago. Four months. A month has about 30 days. Multiply 4 times 30.[M3] That's a lot of days.

That cupcake was really old. I know what you're thinking. You might think a green cupcake is totally normal. What you don't know is

Caterpillar

that when Carmela's mom gave out those cupcakes four months ago, they were yellow and lemon flavored. This cupcake looked green and <u>caterpillar</u>-flavored. That's what mold does to a cupcake.

Chris thought about it. For a few days, the kids had been saying that something smelled bad in the classroom. At some point, they were all going to find out what was stinking up the room.

Have you ever smelled compost? Compost is a pile of rotten food and yard trash that turns into soil.[E4, S11]

Why am I telling you this? Because Chris's feet smelled

KNOWLEDGE NUGGET

S12
E4

Hot compost piles make things degrade (break down) faster than cold ones. Trash turns into soil faster when it's hot.

exactly like compost. They smelled like a pile of rotten, stinking, slimy old trash.

Chris couldn't put his stinky socks into his own book bag. The class would smell them and find out the socks were his. His plan was perfect. The only thing that smelled worse than Chris's socks was that rotten cupcake. All Chris had to do was put the socks in Tuna Tommy's

desk. Everybody would just blame Tuna Tommy for the smell in the room.

Chris took off his right shoe. He <u>paused</u>. It sounded like something was <u>scratching</u> around in the desk. Chris pulled off one of the pink socks. He tried to stick it inside the desk. Before he let go of it, something grabbed it out of his hand. Chris pulled the sock back. He gasped. Something was hanging onto it. You can probably guess what it was.

It was a little brown creature. It had a bite mark on the side of its head.

"Are you gonna eat that?" the creature asked, pointing to the sock. It was the Chicken Nugget Man.

Chris swung the sock around to get the Chicken Nugget Man off of it.

"Weeeeeeeeeeeeee!" the Chicken Nugget Man screamed. He was smiling and laughing. But the Chicken Nugget Man couldn't hold on for very long. He fell off and flew across the room.

Chris quickly put his sock back on. He ran out of the classroom. He screamed and waved his arms

around like a baby in a dirty <u>diaper</u>. In the hall, he ran right into Ms. Bubblebrain. The rest of the class had formed a line behind her. They were coming in from recess. Ms. Bubblebrain held a cup of <u>coffee</u> in her hand. Well, it *used* to be in her hand. It was now all over Brian, another student in the class.

"The coffee! It's burning my eyeballs!" Brian yelled. "I can't see!"

Brian fell on top of Preston. Then Preston fell. The other kids weren't paying attention. They all fell over. They fell one by one, like dominoes. Everybody was on the floor except Chris and Ms. Bubblebrain. There's a reason teachers tell kids to face forward in line.

Ms. Bubblebrain looked back at her class. Kids were crying and rubbing their heads. Tuna Tommy's hands were in Carmela's mouth. Alex's foot was in Smelly Sam's belly.

Belly button

Ms. Bubblebrain sent ten of her twenty students to the school <u>nurse</u>.

Nurse

"Chris Robb!" Ms. Bubblebrain yelled. "What in the name of bacon <u>belly button</u> brownies are you doing?"

What fraction of the class had to go to the nurse? Name a fraction equivalent to that answer. M5

Chris looked up. He was still scared. He was about to tell Ms. Bubblebrain about the Chicken Nugget Man, but he knew she wouldn't believe him.

Can you make a circle (pie) graph showing the percentage (%) of students who had to go to the school nurse? M11

"He don't even have an excuse," Brian yelled.

"Neither do you," Ms. Bubblebrain said to Brian. "We learned about subjects and verbs last week. You can't say 'he don't' in school."[E32]

"Fine," Brian said. "He DOESN'T have an excuse." He then used his shirt to wipe the coffee off his face.

For the love of sweaty bacon soda, answer these questions!
Analysis Question
How would the chapter be different if Chris hadn't run into Ms. Bubblebrain in the hall? E8, E11, E15
Synthesis Question
Can you come up with a way to stop Chris's feet from smelling like a landfill? E15
Evaluation Question
How would you feel if your clumsiness caused half of your class to go to the school nurse? E15, E17

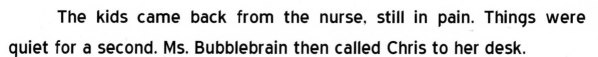

The kids came back from the nurse, still in pain. Things were quiet for a second. Ms. Bubblebrain then called Chris to her desk.

"Chris," she said. "What in the name of grilled termite tacos were you thinking? You were dancing around the hall like a wild animal! I had to send ten students to the nurse! Ten students! And I told you to be outside by 1:35."

"I saw Tuna Tommy's cupcake from Carmela's birthday party," Chris said.

The apostrophe in the word Carmela's is between the a and s because the birthday belongs to Carmela. Where would the apostrophe go if the birthday belonged to Smelly Sam? E31

"Son!" Ms. Bubblebrain yelled. "You are lying through your spinach-covered, fudge-filled teeth. That birthday party was four months ago. There's no way a cupcake is still in that desk. And what smells like sweaty gym sock casserole in here, anyway?"

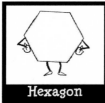
Hexagon

Ms. Bubblebrain looked around the room at the mess Chris had caused. There was no way she could teach with so many kids in pain.

"I'm calling Mr. Turner," she said. "I've had just about enough of this chocolate-covered, cockroach-filled nonsense." She pressed the call button on the wall. It looked like a <u>hexagon</u>.

How many sides does a hexagon have? M9
If it had two more sides, what shape could it be? M9

Chris wanted to kick his desk so far south that it would fall on top of a school in a Mexican <u>valley</u>.SS15 But he knew he would just end up breaking his foot. It was a bad idea, anyway.

Valley

Being angry in school can get you in trouble if you don't know how to calm yourself down. What could Chris do to calm down? SS5, E15, E16

Chris just sat there. Do you think he tried to defend himself? No. Was it fair for Chris to get in trouble?E11 If he tried to explain what had really happened, it might have helped.[SS5] But we all know how Chris feels about trying.[E7]

Chris was angry. It seemed like he was mad at Ms. Bubblebrain, but he was really just mad at himself.

Have you ever acted like you were mad at someone else when you were really just mad at yourself? If so, why? Why do you think Chris acted as if he was mad at his teacher? [E11, E15, E17]

The Chicken Nugget Man was in the corner of the room. He sat inside of a box shaped like a <u>rectangular prism</u>.[M9] He stared at Chris. Chris didn't notice. Something else was on his mind. For the rest of the day,  all Chris could think about was Mr. Turner's warning. If Ms. Bubblebrain had to send Chris to the office one more time, he would be suspended.

Rectangular Prism

After school, Chris got on the bus. It was empty. He finally took off the socks and put them into his book bag.

At home, Chris was worried about getting in trouble for the suspension warning. He was so worried about getting punished that he forgot to take the socks out of his book bag when he got to his room.

For the love of sweaty bacon soda, answer these questions!

Analysis Question
Why did Ms. Bubblebrain send Chris to the office? E10, E11

Synthesis Question
Try to think of something crazy that would have happened if Chris had actually kicked his desk really hard. E15

Evaluation Question
How would you feel if you were Chris and Ms. Bubblebrain sent you to the office after everything that happened in this chapter? Would you have been able to control yourself, or would you have had a temper tantrum? E15, E17

The Anti-Chicken Nugget Task Force

Later that night, Chris's parents were watching TV. The news was on. Chris stared at the phone. He was scared that Ms. Bubblebrain was going to call his parents and tell them what happened at school.

It wasn't worth it to get into trouble that day. He was worried that his teacher would call home. He should have thought about that before he made Smelly Sam put a sock up his nose.[E15] He also felt really bad for all the kids that had to go to the nurse. Sometimes, Chris did things without thinking about what could go wrong later.

Have you ever done something bad without thinking about how much trouble you would get into later? What can Chris do to make sure this doesn't happen again? [E8, E11]

The people on the news were talking about a school bus from a different school. The kids were being loud, and the bus driver couldn't focus on the road. The bus got into a bad accident. A few kids got hurt. That's the reason adults tell kids to behave on the bus.

"Those poor kids," Chris's mom said. "Thank goodness that didn't happen on your bus, Chris! I don't know what we would have done." Chris's mom really cared about kids. She even won a community citizenship award for volunteering to read to homeless kids.[SS1] It's no surprise that she felt so sad for the kids who were on that bus. Chris felt bad for the kids who had been hurt, too.

If you ride the bus, think about the way kids act on it. Is it so loud that the bus driver might not be able to focus on the road? Are you part of the problem? If so, what can you do about it? [E15]

Hallway

A few minutes later, there was a special news report. A man talked about two more children eaten by the Chicken Nugget Man in a school <u>hallway</u>. "Somebody's got to catch that evil Chicken Nugget Man," Chris's mom said. "We can't let him eat any more children!"

President

"Well," Chris's dad said, "that's why the <u>President</u> created the Anti-Chicken Nugget Task Force. That task force makes books that teach kids to stay away from the Chicken Nugget Man. The Task Force keeps us safe. If people like me hadn't voted for our President, we wouldn't even have an Anti-Chicken Nugget Task Force."

Chris's dad really liked the President. Chris's dad always told Chris that voting was one way to help things go the way you want them to. He said voting was his civic responsibility. Chris had no idea what that meant.[SS3]

Using adults to find the Chicken Nugget Man was a bad idea. Kids were the only ones that ever saw him. The President was looking for smart kids, and those kids would help catch the Chicken Nugget Man.

The news was about a new test that kids all over the country would have to take. They called the one for North Carolina the End of Grade (EOG) test. The kids with the best scores would get to join the Anti-Chicken Nugget Task Force. The kid with the highest score would be in charge of the Task Force. That kid would be famous!

Chris listened to the people on the news talk about how the Chicken Nugget Man must be stopped. Even the weatherman agreed with them!

Is the news on TV discussing different opinions about the Chicken Nugget Man, or is it only sharing one opinion? Is it trying to inform or persuade? E18

For the next few nights, Chris couldn't sleep very well. Each night, he just stared at the moon from his bedroom window. He really didn't want Ms. Bubblebrain to talk to his parents about his behavior.

On President's Day, there was no school. It was a holiday. The holiday

KNOWLEDGE NUGGET

S16

S17

S14

The moon goes through a pattern of shape changes. It starts in a phase called the New Moon, then goes to the First Quarter and looks like a half-circle. It looks brighter until it becomes a Full Moon. In the Last Quarter, it's a half-circle again. You can use a calendar to track the moon's movements.

used to just celebrate George Washington's birthday. Now it celebrates all of our presidents.[SS6] Chris spent the whole day doing chores. It was his role at home. He did his chores and his homework until bedtime.

It had been a few days and Ms. Bubblebrain still hadn't called, but Chris was still worried. He hadn't slept well in almost a week.

Have you ever felt like Chris? Have you ever had trouble sleeping because you were worried about getting in trouble for something you did? [E15]

KNOWLEDGE NUGGET

[SS7] [SS9]

Chris's role (the part he plays) at home is to do chores and be a learner. Kids in some countries have to work and earn money for their families.

For the love of sweaty bacon soda, answer these questions!
Analysis Question
How would this chapter be different if Ms. Bubblebrain had actually called Chris's parents? [E8, E11, E15]
Synthesis Question
If you were chosen to be part of the Anti-Chicken Nugget Task Force, what would you do? Would you try to catch the Chicken Nugget Man? If so, how would you do it? [E15]
Evaluation Question
Do you think it's a good idea to have kids join the Anti-Chicken Nugget Task Force? Why or why not? [E11, E15, E17]

Can't You Do Anything Right?

In your opinion, does Chris care about school? Do you think he wants to do well in school? What have you read that makes you believe that? E10, E11

"Children! For the love of lizard-filled lasagna, settle down!" Ms. Bubblebrain shouted. She pulled out a book called *The Stages of a Plant's Life*. "Have a seat. The other day, we learned about star patterns. We learned that they look like they move every night but they don't.[S18] But we're done with star patterns. Today, we're going to talk about plants."

Ms. Bubblebrain told the class that soil is made of humus, clay, and sand.[S10] Chris didn't listen. In fact, he did the exact opposite of active listening.[E14] He wasn't facing his teacher. He wasn't asking questions. He was just daydreaming about a flying purple hamster that saved the world from evil. He had a hard time with science, but he used to like it. In fact, he used to like every subject in school.

It all changed after the first grade. That's when Chris started having trouble paying attention. It made teachers think he didn't care.

Chris wanted to get good grades, but for some reason, he couldn't pay attention. His teachers thought he didn't care. His parents thought he didn't care. They were always talking about his big sister.

"Can't you do anything right?" they would ask Chris. "Why can't you be more like your sister?"

Chris never stopped caring. But he did stop trying.

Preston took notes while Ms. Bubblebrain talked about the things people do to change the land in order to help plants grow. Chris was still daydreaming.

KNOWLEDGE NUGGET

SS16

People change the land to help crops grow. They clear it, turn the soil, plant seeds, and dig paths to water plants. We do many things to land to make it work for us. We mine it, make lakes, and even build tunnels!

For the love of sweaty bacon soda, answer these questions!

Analysis Question

How is Chris's daydream in this chapter similar to a daydream he had earlier in the story durin class? If you can't remember the earlier daydream, go back and find it in chapter 10. E8, E16

Synthesis Question

Create a silly way to remember the words humus, clay, and sand. Use the first letters of each word (H, C, and S) to make a group of silly words. For example, hot caterpillar sandwich. Then, whenever you need to remember the things soil is made of, you can think about your silly words and use the first letters in those words to help you remember humus, clay, and sand. S10

Evaluation Question

How do you think Chris feels when his parents compare him to his sister? Use a complete sentence. Try starting with "It probably makes Chris want to..." or "Chris probably feels like..." E8, E15, E17, E33

16 THE EXPLOSIVE SNEEZE

You are about to learn more about Alex in this chapter. Pay attention! E7

Sneeze

From the back of the room, Carmela <u>sneezed</u> so loudly that everybody thought the school exploded. Ms. Bubblebrain threw her papers into the air and hid under her desk.

"Everybody duck!" Ms. Bubblebrain screamed. "It's the Chicken Nugget Man! He's coming to eat us!"

Smelly Sam cried for his mommy. Everybody looked around for the Chicken Nugget Man, but he wasn't there.

It was a loud sneeze, even for Carmela. Tuna Tommy was the only kid not hiding under a desk. He sat two feet away from Carmela. That's about the length of your arm.M8

Tuna Tommy was rubbing the back of his head. "Gross!" he yelled. "It's all over me! It's sticky and slimy and gross!" The back of his head was covered in green goo.

"Exclamatory sentence!" Alex said.[E33]

Alex always did that. He used to be the smartest kid in the class. One day somebody stole his lunch. It had a tuna sandwich in it. He ran around the halls looking for it. His shoe fell off. There's a reason teachers tell kids to tie their shoes. Alex ran right into a pole, a metal pole. The sound was almost as loud as one of Carmela's sneezes. It rang all over the school. Ms. Bubblebrain even thought the bell had rung.

Alex had to see the doctor that day. Running into that pole messed up Alex's memory. Each day, he would remember only one of Ms. Bubblebrain's lessons. But that one lesson was always from months earlier. That's all he would think about and talk about.

The day Carmela sneezed was the day Alex remembered the four types of sentences. That lesson was really old. Alex talked about the types of sentences all day. The good news is that he would forget that lesson by the end of the day. The bad news is that he would talk about a different one the next day. It was annoying. It was almost as annoying as the stinky food in Tuna Tommy's desk.

Crawl

Ms. Bubblebrain <u>crawled</u> out from under her desk. She fixed her hair.

Tuna Tommy ran to the restroom. Carmela felt bad for sneezing all over him. The whole class started talking.

"Settle down," Ms. Bubblebrain said.

"Imperative sentence!" Alex said.[E33]

"Stop saying that!" Carmela shouted.

"Imperative and exclamatory," Alex said.[E33]

"Carmela, you know you're supposed to ignore him when he does that," Ms. Bubblebrain said. "Actually, you should just ignore him when he does anything."

SOIL
Wilting

Flower

"Declarative," Alex said quietly.[E33] He slowly dropped his head. He looked kind of like a <u>flower wilting</u> because the soil was too dry.[S1]

For the love of sweaty bacon soda, answer these questions!

Analysis Question
How is Alex similar to Chris? E11, E15

Synthesis Question
Can you make up a machine that would fix Alex's memory problem? How would it work? What would it do to help Alex remember more than one of Ms. Bubblebrain's lessons at a time? E15

Evaluation Question
Do you think that the way the class treats Alex is fair? Do you think he is as strong as Smelly Sam and Tuna Tommy? Why do you believe that? E11, E15, E16

17
BARBECUE SAUCE

"Different soils take in water at different speeds," Ms. Bubblebrain said.[S8] The kids looked bored. Some were asleep.

"If you don't pay attention," Ms. Bubblebrain said, "how will you get the best scores on the EOG test? Some other kid will get to work with the Anti-Chicken Nugget Task Force. The world needs smart leaders who can come up with great ideas to change the world.[S4] This is your chance to show people how smart you are. There are lots of adults who'd do anything to get to work with the Task Force. You should feel lucky. Now open your books to the

KNOWLEDGE NUGGET

[SS2]

Milton Hunt is a leader known for his work as the mayor of Pembroke, NC. He brought businesses to the city and worked to gain rights for Native Americans in the area.

page that is equal to 8 x 3. If you have trouble, just add 8 + 8 + 8. Then turn to that page.^{M3} We need to talk about plants."

Ms. Bubblebrain says leaders are smart. What are some other qualities of good leaders? ^{SS4}

There was a noise at the back of the room. Something scratched the floor. Ms. Bubblebrain stopped teaching. She was scared. You could see it in her eyes. The kids were scared, too. They were all thinking the same thing. They were afraid it was the Chicken Nugget Man.

"I don't want to be eated," Brian cried.

"Eaten," Ms. Bubblebrain whispered. "Eated isn't a word."^{E37} She was still staring at the back of the room.

Barbecue

The students in the back moved their desks forward. Ms. Bubblebrain grabbed a bottle of <u>barbecue</u> sauce.

Why do you think Ms. Bubblebrain grabbed the barbecue sauce? ^{E8, E15}

The noises finally stopped. Ms. Bubblebrain told the class not to worry. She told them to start thinking about plants.

Chris didn't want to think about plants. He failed the first plant test a few weeks ago. The test was about the things that change how many seeds a plant makes.

What are some questions you still have about the Chicken Nugget Man? [E7, E8]

The answers were nutrients, pollination, sunlight, and water.[S4] Those things can change the number of seeds a plant makes. Chris didn't even know that plants made seeds. He thought seeds were made in a factory in Japan. He wasn't trying to pay attention to that lesson that

KNOWLEDGE NUGGET

SS20

Plants love light. They always grow towards it. If you put a light beside a plant, the stem will grow sideways toward the light! Plants grow in the direction of light.

day. He never really tried to pay attention. By this point, you know that he never really tried to do anything.

Chris still had to answer the question about what changes the number of seeds a plant makes. So what was his answer? He wrote "batteries." Poor Chris, he actually thought that plants were machines.

He decided that plants were boring. He raised his hand and felt his triceps moving.[S23]

KNOWLEDGE NUGGET

S2

Factories in Japan and all over the world divide work between many people. If they are making a car, some people spend all day just making engine parts, and others might spend all day putting those parts together.

"Ms. Butterbuns," Chris asked, "may I please get some water?"

"Chris, my name is Ms. Bubblebrain. And you have to answer a question before I let you go."

She touched her chin. Chris lowered his head.

"What's the opposite of multiplication?"[M3] Ms. Bubblebrain asked. She was always asking questions. Her students knew that if they wanted something, they would have to answer a question first.

Chris didn't know the answer.

Ms. Bubblebrain gave him another chance. "Is it about $30°$, $70°$, or $110°$ Fahrenheit in this room right now?"[M8]

"B," Chris said.

"That wasn't a multiple choice question," Ms. Bubblebrain said. She was so angry that Chris thought her nose was going to explode.

If you add up all three temperatures (30, 70, and 110), what do you get? [M2, M6]

"Okay, last try," she said. "Give me an interrogative sentence."[E33]

"What's an interrogative sentence?" Chris asked.

"Go ahead, Chris," Ms. Bubblebrain said, "but be fast. We'll be talking about the stages of a plant's life. I'm going to call on you to answer a question about that when you get back."

Chris had no idea why Ms. Bubblebrain decided to let him go. He didn't know that he had actually given her an example of an interrogative sentence. Sometimes people just get lucky. Ms. Bubblebrain knew that Chris got lucky. She just didn't want to make him feel bad since he couldn't answer any of her questions.

KNOWLEDGE NUGGET

SS2

You learned about leaders in this chapter. Another important leader is a former president named Lyndon Johnson who signed civil rights and voting rights laws, giving rights to many African Americans.

For the love of sweaty bacon soda, answer these questions!

Analysis Question

What do you think would have happened if the Chicken Nugget Man had come out of his hiding place and the kids had seen him? E8, E11, E15

Synthesis Question

Can you create a silly way to remember nutrients, pollination, sunlight, and water? Use the first letters of each word again (N, P, S, and W) to make a silly group of words. For example, Neon Penguins Smell Weird. Then, when you need to remember the things that affect the number of seeds a plant makes, you can remember your silly words and use the first letters to remember nutrients, pollination, sunlight, and water. S2, S4

Evaluation Question

Do you think that Ms. Bubblebrain's speech about the smart leaders was inspiring? What could she have said to get the kids more excited about passing the test? E15, E17

A Burp to Remember

18

Ms. Bubblebrain put down the bottle of barbecue sauce. "Singers aren't the only ones who get stages," she said. "Plants are renewable resources and they have stages, too." She waited for the class to laugh. Nobody laughed. Nobody even smiled. It just wasn't funny. "You kids are as boring as banana bunny burgers," she said.

KNOWLEDGE NUGGET

SS21

Renewable things can be made again. They are one type of resource. Other types are nonrenewable (like gold) which can't be made again quickly, human (workers), and capital (tools or buildings).

When authors compare one thing to another using the words *like* or *as*, they are creating a simile. "As boring as banana bunny burgers" is an example of a simile. Ew, gross. [E10]

Chris left the room. Ms. Bubblebrain started talking about pollen.

"Pollen sticks to bees as they go from flower to flower searching for food," she said. "It then brushes off onto other flowers when the bees land."[S3, S5] It's too bad Chris wasn't there. He didn't know a thing about pollen. He thought bees were allergic to pollen. He actually thought their sneezes blew pollen from flower to flower.

KNOWLEDGE NUGGET [S4]

Most plants need pollen to reproduce and make seeds.

Now that you know what a simile is, can you find one on this page?[E3, E10]

KNOWLEDGE NUGGET [S6]

Seed properties include size, shape, color, and texture. Seeds are protected by seed coats.

In the hallway, Chris heard weird noises from the water fountain. The noises were as loud

Intercom

as the time Mr. Turner burped over the <u>intercom</u>. That happened while he was doing the morning message.

"Good morn- *BURRRRRRRP!*"

Even Ms. Bubblebrain laughed. How often do you get to hear your principal burp over the intercom? Students would sometimes give him a soda in the morning just to hear him burp again.

Chris got close to the fountain, and the noises stopped. He leaned down. He was about to swallow a gulp of water. That's when he saw a tiny hand. Chris saw his life flash before him. It didn't last long. He was only eight.

For the love of sweaty bacon soda, answer these questions!

Analysis Question

Why do you think Ms. Bubblebrain tried to tell a joke at the beginning of the chapter? Think about it. You might want to reread that part. There's a reason she wanted to make the kids laugh. E8, E11, E15

Synthesis Question

We know that pollen sticks to bees and falls onto other flowers as they fly around. Can you come up with a different way for bees to put pollen on a whole bunch of flowers? Be creative! S5, E15

Evaluation Question

If you could tell Chris what to do as soon as he saw that tiny hand, what would you say? E8, E15, E17

I'm Actually Talking to a Chunk of Chicken

19

"Don't scream," whispered a tiny little voice from the cracks in the water fountain.

Chris backed away, spitting out the water. Guess who was walking by right then?[E8] It was Tuna Tommy, on his way to the restroom again. Let's just say it wasn't his day. The water that Chris spat out hit Tuna Tommy in the face. He was dripping from head to toe, and his hair was sticking straight out.

"Why do people keep doing this to me?" Tuna Tommy yelled. He ran into the restroom. Water dripped from his chin.

What caused Tuna Tommy to ask "Why do people keep doing this to me?" [E10, E11]
Do you know what it's like to be in his shoes? Have you ever had such a bad day? [E15, E17]

The hallway was empty again. Chris looked into the cracks in the water fountain. Something was moving inside. He knew just what it was. He jumped away.

Chipmunk

"Don't eat me," Chris said. He was so scared that it came out as a whisper.

A voice came out of the fountain. It sounded like a little <u>chipmunk</u>.

It was the Chicken Nugget Man.

"I don't eat humans," he said. He then looked at Chris's feet.

Why do you think the Chicken Nugget Man looked at Chris's feet? [E8, E10, E15]

"Yeah right," Chris said. "You're just going to make up some lie about how your body makes its own food. Then when I believe you, you'll take a bite out of my head."

KNOWLEDGE NUGGET [S15]

Standing in the sunlight, your shadow is longer early and late in the day because the sun is at a lower angle.

"Do I look like a leaf?" the Chicken Nugget Man asked. "I don't use sunlight to make my own food."[S1]

Chris remembered learning that in science class. It was weird. He actually remembered something he had learned in school.

"You didn't tell your teacher that you saw me in that desk," the Chicken Nugget Man said. "You helped me, Chris. And I can help you, too."

"You eat children," Chris said. "I don't trust you. I'm not helping you."

"They just tell you that so you'll get scared," the Chicken Nugget Man said. "It's like those books they make you read about me. The Anti-

KNOWLEDGE NUGGET

SS28 SS29

You've probably heard many fictional stories like one about Paul Bunyan, a make-believe giant. Stories say he dug holes that created huge bodies of water.

Chicken Nugget Task Force wrote them to scare you. They aren't true. They're fiction, not fact."[E10, E13]

Chris looked up at one of the signs on the wall. It said, "Chicken Nuggets Banned by Federal Law." Those signs were everywhere.

He thought about how weird this was. He was actually talking to a chicken nugget. But it wasn't just weird. It was scary. What if it was a trick?

Just then, Chris remembered what his teacher had said about muscles and joints. They help the body move.[S22, S23]

He was glad

KNOWLEDGE NUGGET

S21

There are 3 types of joints. Gliding joints help bones move in all directions and are in the hand and wrist. Ball-and-socket joints allow bones to move back and forth, in a circle, and side to side. Hinge joints allow bones to move back and forth in one direction (just like doors).

to have those joints and muscles. How else could he get away from Chicken Nugget Man?

"Joints and muscles," he whispered to himself. "That's the second lesson I remembered today!" Something about the Chicken Nugget Man helped him remember things. And with that thought, he used those joints and muscles to get moving. Chris passed the restroom. Tuna Tommy was still inside trying to get the water off his shirt.

In the word "he's," what is the name of that little mark between the e and the s? What two words make up the word "he's?" [E31]

Chris walked toward the office. The Chicken Nugget Man knew that's where he was going. But to Chris's surprise, he didn't follow him.

Stop and think about it. What might happen if Chris tries to tell Mr. Turner about the Chicken Nugget Man? [E8, E15]

"It's okay," the Chicken Nugget Man yelled from the fountain. "I shouldn't have expected you to give me a chance."

KNOWLEDGE NUGGET

SS28 SS29

The Chicken Nugget Man says the stories about him are fictional. You may have heard of a fictional story about a boy named Hunter Bickford. According to the story, Hunter and his mom (a teacher) created an entire North Carolina community. We sometimes tell fictional stories to show pride for things. In Hunter's case, it was a community.

For the love of sweaty bacon soda, answer these questions!

Analysis Question
How is what happened to Tuna Tommy in the hallway similar to what happened to Bobby Rough on the bus earlier in the book? E8, E15, E16

Synthesis Question
What could Chris do to find out if the Chicken Nugget Man was telling the truth? E8, E15

Evaluation Question
If you were Chris, would you believe the Chicken Nugget Man, or would you believe all of the stories you had read and heard about him eating children? E8, E15, E17

GET BUSY LIVING OR GET BUSY FRYING

20

Can you think of a time when you had trouble trusting someone because of something you heard about him or her? [E15, E17]

Chris stopped to think as he walked toward the office. He remembered all the scary things he'd heard about the Chicken Nugget Man.

"You're right. Nobody will believe me," Chris said. "Nobody will ever believe me. That's why I never try. But I don't need your help. I have to get back to class. I need to make up something about plant stages."

Chris started walking back down the hall. He didn't look back at the water fountain. He didn't even look back at the Chicken Nugget Man. He passed a political map. It had lines between cities and states.[SS13] Each city and state started with a capital letter.[E31]

"Survival, growth, and reproduction," the Chicken Nugget Man said.

"What?" Chris asked. He turned around.

"The stages of a plant's life," the Chicken Nugget Man said. "Plants go through three stages. They're called survival, growth, and reproduction."[S3]

Can you remember which type of map shows the names of cities, states, and boundaries? [SS13, E8]
Can you remember the three stages of a plant's life? Reread the page if you need to. [S3, E8]

"What do *you* know about plants?" Chris asked.

"I know a lot more than you think," the Chicken Nugget Man said. "And I know what it's like to feel like everybody's out to get you. You humans try to catch me. You try to fry me in burning hot oil. You don't care that I'm a living creature. We can get out and run away or fry in the oil. It's just like the choice you have, Chris. Get busy living, or get busy frying."

Chris just stared at the water fountain.

"Survival, growth, and reproduction,"[S3] the Chicken Nugget Man said. He crawled back into the tiny cracks in the water fountain. There were four cracks on each of the three sides.

If y is the total number of cracks in the water fountain, what multiplication problem shows four cracks on each of the three sides: $4 \times 4 = y$, $4 \times 3 = y$, or $4 \times 4 \times 4 = y$? [M3, M16]

Chris stared at the water fountain. He opened the door to his classroom.

"Get busy living, or get busy frying," he thought.

For the love of sweaty bacon soda, answer these questions!

Analysis Question
What would have happened if Chris had yelled for help? There's no wrong answer to this one. Use your imagination. [E8, E15]

Synthesis Question
Can you think of a silly group of words starting with S,G, and R that can help you remember that survival, growth, and reproduction are the stages of a plant's life? For example: Slimy, Green, Roaches. [S3]

Evaluation Question
Do you believe that Chris is spending his time trying to really live and enjoy life (getting busy living,) or is he just letting bad things happen to him without trying to make it better? [E11, E15]

How has your opinion (feelings) about the Chicken Nugget Man changed since the beginning of the book? [E7, E10, E12]

"Well, shake my pepper and call me beef cake," Ms. Bubblebrain said. "Look who took so long at the water fountain. You missed our whole lesson about plant stages. I know one student who is going to be sad when someone else gets to work with the Anti-Chicken Nugget Task Force." She told Chris that he needed to start trying. She told him that he needed to start caring about school.

That was when everything changed for Chris Robb. He knew he wasn't good at reading. He knew he wasn't good at math. He knew he wasn't good at remembering things. The main idea here is that he knew he wasn't good at anything.[E11] But for the first time, he wanted something badly enough to do something about it.

He wanted Ms. Bubblebrain to know that he could remember something he learned. He wanted the other students to stop laughing at him. He wanted his parents to know that his sister wasn't better than he was. Most of all, Chris wanted to prove he could pass the EOG.

What are some words you would use to describe what kind of person Chris is? How has your opinion of him changed? E8, E15

So on that hot afternoon, Chris looked his teacher straight in the eye. He took a deep breath. "Ms. Bubblebrain," Chris said, "plants go through three stages: survival, growth, and reproduction."[S3]

The room was silent. Ms. Bubblebrain stared at Chris. Her mouth opened so wide that a family of flying gorillas could have flown inside. Her jaw dropped to the floor. Then she said it, one word at a time. It was the longest, grossest food she had ever named.

Skeleton

"Holy peanut-butter-and-donkey lasagna-covered, spinach-pretzel-filled, beef-and-boxer-shorts donuts with brown sugar <u>skeletons</u> and banana-covered battery frosting! You actually remembered something!"

Try to reread that last paragraph (the one with the list of really gross food) clearly, with expression, and without making mistakes. It might take several tries, but you'll get really good at it! Then, read it aloud with expression to someone. E6, E21

For the love of sweaty bacon soda, answer these questions!

Analysis Question
If all of this had happened in the 1st grade instead of the 3rd grade, how would the story be different? Would Chris still have trouble remembering things by the time he got to the 3rd grade? E8, E15, E17

Synthesis Question
The Chicken Nugget Man says, "Get busy living or get busy frying." Adults have a similar saying, "Get busy living, or get busy dying." Make up your own silly saying! For example, "Get busy passing, or get busy failing...get busy giving your all, or get busy giving up." Try it: Get busy _____, or get busy _____. E15

Evaluation Question
How would you feel if people thought you weren't smart and you finally proved them wrong? Use a complete sentence like, "I would feel like _____" or "I would feel so _____ that I would _____." E15, E17, E33

On the bus that afternoon, Chris had a seat all to himself. Nobody sat near him. He was tired, so he leaned on the window. That's when he saw the Chicken Nugget Man stick his head out of his book bag. Chris was too tired to talk. He thought it was just a bad dream.

"We're making a deal," the Chicken Nugget Man whispered. He looked around. He wanted to make sure nobody was looking. "You feed me. I'll teach you," he said.

"What?" Chris asked.

"I'll fill your brain. You fill my tummy," the Chicken Nugget Man said.

Chris couldn't keep his eyes open. If this was a trick, Chris was about to be the main dish at the Chicken Nugget Man's next dinner party. He thought about what the Chicken Nugget Man had said earlier,

"Get busy living, or get busy frying." Chris really did have that choice. He could try to make his life better and get busy living. His other choice was to just sit back and let bad things happen to him. It kind of made sense to just get busy living.

Half of a pink sock hung out of the Chicken Nugget Man's mouth. Chris had left that sock in his bag for several days. He had totally forgotten about it. That's why his book bag had smelled so bad all week!

"What kind of food do you eat?" Chris asked. The Chicken Nugget Man didn't answer. Instead, he swallowed the sock in one big gulp, burping up the purple glitter. That answered that question!

"Chris," the Chicken Nugget Man said, rubbing his tummy, "you're going to pass that test. And I'm going to help you."

"But I'm so bad at reading," Chris said. "I mean, I turn pages when I finish them. Several pages later, I realize I haven't been paying attention to the story. Something's wrong with me. I can't learn stuff."

"I'll help you with that," the Chicken Nugget Man said. "Everyone can learn. Even you. Especially you."

"And math. Don't get me started with math. I just don't know how to think that fast. Ms. Bubblebooger talks so fast and--"

"Chris, I'll help you with that."

"And all the kids that make fun of me. I can't think straight when I'm worried about being teased. And I keep getting in trouble and--"

"Chris, I'll help you."

Chris stopped talking. He thought about Mr. Wit. He was the one adult at school who actually gave Chris a chance. Chris couldn't help but think about the Chicken Nugget Man, who was also willing to help him. Things didn't seem so hopeless anymore.

Chris's eyelids closed. It wasn't just because he was tired. It was as if a heavy weight had been lifted from his shoulders. He could rest now. Things were going to be okay.

The bus driver woke Chris up at his stop. "Son, you okay?" the bus driver asked in a kind voice. "Last stop. This one's yours."

Chris jumped out of his seat. "I didn't do anything!" he yelled. "Just don't make me smell your shoe!" He thought he was going to get blamed for something again.

Chris quickly realized that the bus driver was just being nice and waking him up. Chris worried that he was going to get in trouble for yelling and being so jumpy.

"It's okay," the bus driver said. "You're not in trouble. It's just your stop. Time to go home. And look, I'm sorry I yelled at you that day. I just get worried that one of you will get hurt when it gets so loud on the bus. I lose my temper sometimes. Now go on, kid. Have a good weekend."

Chris walked to the front of the bus. He noticed something taped to the bus driver's side dashboard. It was a picture of a little girl.

"That's my little girl," the bus driver said.

She looked familiar. It wasn't until he got off the bus that Chris realized that he had seen her before. She was on the news a while ago. She was one of the kids who got hurt in a bus accident because the kids were acting up.

Chris felt horrible. All this time, he thought the bus driver was just a mean old man who didn't like kids. He'd thought he was about to be blamed for something else when the bus driver woke him up. Chris hadn't given the guy a chance. He just assumed that the driver was out to get him. And he was wrong.

Before he got home, Chris looked down at his book bag. The Chicken Nugget Man was gone. Little pieces of purple glitter were all that remained.

* * *

So it seemed as if the only thing the Chicken Nugget Man ever attacked was a pink sock. But that wasn't the full story. He had attacked Chris's fears. He had attacked Chris's laziness. And he had attacked the belief that Chris couldn't learn.

Chris had learned that he needed to give people a chance. More importantly, he needed to give himself a chance, a chance to turn his life around. And whether the Chicken Nugget Man returned or not, that was exactly what Chris was going to do.

For the next few days there was something different about Chris Robb. He wasn't getting in trouble every day. He stopped asking to leave class. He stopped hiding when Ms. Bubblebrain asked questions.

Nobody could explain it. The kids didn't know what to do. It was harder to make fun of him now. After all, Chris Robb was trying.

For the love of broiled beetle bologna, do some writing!

Do some research using the Internet to find out who invented the chicken nugget and how it became so famous. You can also talk to people and discuss why they like chicken nuggets. Or if you want, you can research the history of barbecue sauce. It might have something to do with Christopher Columbus! Organize your thoughts using a list or a KWL chart (what you _know_, what you _want_ to know, and what you _learned_). Figure out your purpose (why you are writing and whether it is to inform or entertain). Then, create a rough draft using good handwriting (try cursive). Make it at least 3 paragraphs. E20, E22, E24, E25, E26, E38

Try to write a poem, a letter or a story about chicken nuggets or BBQ sauce. If you write a letter make sure you follow the rules for letter writing. Try not to use first grade words like good or bad. Use big words and be descriptive! Check your spelling using a dictionary. Type your final draft on a computer. Share your final copy with your class or a few adults. E5, E23, E27, E29, E28, E30, E34, E36

TO BE continued...

Be careful around those water fountains.
You never know what might be inside.

Thanks for reading!

Visit our website at www.chickennuggetman.com
for Chicken Nugget Man info, discussions with the author, a chance to share your opinion
about the book, and more! You can also write letters to the author! Send letters to:
Chicken Nugget Man, PO Box 2428, Chapel Hill, NC 27515-2428.

THE NORTH CAROLINA STANDARD COURSE OF STUDY

REFERENCE NUMBER	SUBJECT	NC ID#	DESCRIPTION OF STANDARD (COURSE CONCEPT)	USED
			ENGLISH/LANGUAGE ARTS *Skills in this subject area have a check in the last column if they are addressed in the book*	
E1	English	1.01	Apply phonics and structural analysis to decode words (e.g., roots, suffixes, prefixes, less common vowel patterns, syllable breaks).	✓
E2	English	1.02	Apply meanings of common prefixes and suffixes to decode words in text to assist comprehension.	✓
E3	English	1.03	Integrate prior experiences and all sources of information in the text (graphophonic, syntactic, and semantic) when reading orally and silently.	✓
E4	English	1.04	Increase sight vocabulary, reading vocabulary, and writing vocabulary through: wide reading, word study, listening, discussion, book talks, book clubs, seminars, viewing, role play, studying author's craft.	✓
E5	English	1.05	Use word reference materials (e.g., dictionary, glossary) to confirm decoding skills, verify spelling, and extend meanings of words.	✓
E6	English	1.06	Read independently daily from self-selected materials (consistent with the student's independent reading level) to: increase fluency, build background knowledge, extend vocabulary.	✓
E7	English	2.01	Use metacognitive strategies to comprehend text (e.g., reread, read ahead, ask for help, adjust reading speed, question, paraphrase, retell).	✓

REFERENCE NUMBER	SUBJECT	NC ID#	DESCRIPTION OF STANDARD (COURSE CONCEPT)	USED
E8	English	2.02	Interact with the text before, during, and after reading, listening, or viewing by: setting a purpose, previewing the text, making predictions, asking questions, locating information for specific purposes, making connections, using story structure and text organization to comprehend.	✓
E9	English	2.03	Read a variety of texts, including: fiction (short stories, novels, fantasies, fairy tales, fables), nonfiction (biographies, letters, articles, procedures and instructions, charts, maps), poetry (proverbs, riddles, limericks, simple poems), drama (skits, plays).	✓
E10	English	2.04	Identify and interpret elements of fiction and nonfiction and support by referencing the text to determine the: author's purpose, plot, conflict, sequence, resolution, lesson and/or message, main idea and supporting details, cause and effect, fact and opinion, point of view (author and character), author's use of figurative language (e.g., simile, metaphor, imagery).	✓
E11	English	2.05	Draw conclusions, make generalizations, and gather support by referencing the text.	✓
E12	English	2.06	Summarize main idea(s) from written or spoken texts using succinct language.	✓
E13	English	2.07	Explain choice of reading materials congruent with purposes (e.g., solving problems, making decisions).	✓

Reference Number	Subject	NC ID#	Description of Standard (Course Concept)	Used
E14	English	2.08	Listen actively by: facing the speaker, making eye contact, asking questions to clarify the message, asking questions to gain additional information and ideas.	√
E15	English	3.01	Respond to fiction, nonfiction, poetry, and drama using interpretive, critical, and evaluative processes by: considering the differences among genres, relating plot, setting, and characters to own experiences and ideas, considering main character's point of view, participating in creative interpretations, making inferences and drawing conclusions about characters and events, reflecting on learning, gaining new insights, and identifying areas for further study.	√
E16	English	3.02	Identify and discuss similarities and differences in events, characters, concepts and ideas within and across selections and support them by referencing the text.	√
E17	English	3.03	Use text and own experiences to verify facts, concepts, and ideas.	√
E18	English	3.04	Make informed judgments about television productions.	√
E19	English	3.05	Analyze, compare and contrast printed and visual information (e.g., graphs, charts, maps).	√
E20	English	3.06	Conduct research for assigned and self-selected projects (with assistance) from a variety of sources (e.g., print and non-print texts, artifacts, people, libraries, databases, computer networks).	√
E21	English	4.01	Read aloud grade-appropriate text with fluency, comprehension, and expression.	√

Reference Number	Subject	NC ID#	Description of Standard (Course Concept)	Used
E22	English	4.02	Use oral and written language to: present information in a sequenced, logical manner. discuss; sustain conversation on a topic; share information and ideas; recount or narrate; answer open-ended questions; report information on a topic; explain own learning.	√
E23	English	4.03	Share written and oral products in a variety of ways (e.g., author's chair, book making, publications, discussions, presentations).	√
E24	English	4.04	Use planning strategies (with assistance) to generate topics and to organize ideas (e.g., drawing, mapping, discussing, listing).	√
E25	English	4.05	Identify (with assistance) the purpose, the audience, and the appropriate form for the oral or written task.	√
E26	English	4.06	Compose a draft that conveys major ideas and maintains focus on the topic by using preliminary plans.	√
E27	English	4.07	Compose a variety of fiction, nonfiction, poetry, and drama selections using self-selected topics and forms (e.g., poems, simple narratives, short reports, learning logs, letters, notes, directions, instructions).	√
E28	English	4.08	Focus reflection and revision (with assistance) on target elements by: clarifying ideas; adding descriptive words and phrases; sequencing events and ideas; combining short, related sentences; strengthening word choice.	√
E29	English	4.09	Produce work that follows the conventions of particular genres (e.g., personal narrative, short report, friendly letter, directions and instructions).	√
E30	English	4.1	Explore technology as a tool to create a written product.	√

REFERENCE NUMBER	SUBJECT	NC ID#	DESCRIPTION OF STANDARD (COURSE CONCEPT)	USED
E31	English	5.01	Use correct capitalization (e.g., geographical place names, holidays, special events, titles) and punctuation (e.g., commas in greetings, dates, city and state; underlining book titles; periods after initials and abbreviated titles; apostrophes in contractions).	✓
E32	English	5.02	Use correct subject/verb agreement.	✓
E33	English	5.03	Demonstrate understanding by using a variety of complete sentences (declarative, imperative, interrogative, and exclamatory) in writing and speaking.	✓
E34	English	5.04	Compose two or more paragraphs with: topic sentences; supporting details; appropriate, logical sequence; sufficient elaboration.	✓
E35	English	5.05	Use a number of strategies for spelling (e.g., sound patterns, visual patterns, silent letters, less common letter groupings).	✓
E36	English	5.06	Proofread own writing for spelling and correct most misspellings independently with reference to resources (e.g., dictionaries, glossaries, word walls).	✓
E37	English	5.07	Edit (with assistance) to use conventions of written language and format.	✓
E38	English	5.08	Create readable documents with legible handwriting (manuscript and cursive).	✓
MATHEMATICS *Skills in this subject area have a check in the last column if they are addressed in the book*				
M1	Math	1.01	Develop number sense for whole numbers through 9,999. a. Connect model, number word, and number using a variety of representations. b. Build understanding of place value (ones through thousands). c. Compare and order.	✓
M2	Math	1.02	Develop fluency with multi-digit addition and subtraction through 9,999 using: a. Strategies for adding and subtracting numbers. b. Estimation of sums and differences in appropriate situations. c. Relationships between operations.	✓

Reference Number	Subject	NC ID#	Description of Standard (Course Concept)	Used
M3	Math	1.03	Develop fluency with multiplication from 1x1 to 12x12 and division up to two-digit by one-digit numbers using: a. Strategies for multiplying and dividing numbers. b. Estimation of products and quotients in appropriate situations. c. Relationships between operations.	√
M4	Math	1.04	Use basic properties (identity, commutative, associative, order of operations) for addition, subtraction, multiplication, and division.	√
M5	Math	1.05	Use area/region and set models of fractions to explore part-whole relationships. a. Represent fractions concretely and symbolically (halves, fourths, thirds, sixths, eighths). b. Compare and order fractions (halves, fourths, thirds, sixths, eighths) using models and benchmark numbers (zero, one-half, one); describe comparisons. c. Model and describe common equivalents, especially relationships among halves, fourths, and eighths, and thirds and sixths. d. Understand that the fractional relationships that occur between zero and one also occur between every two consecutive whole numbers. e. Understand and use mixed numbers and their equivalent fraction forms.	√
M6	Math	1.06	Develop flexibility in solving problems by selecting strategies and using mental computation, estimation, calculators or computers, and paper and pencil.	√
M7	Math	2.01	Solve problems using measurement concepts and procedures involving: a. Elapsed time. b. Equivalent measures within the same measurement system.	√
M8	Math	2.02	Estimate and measure using appropriate units. a. Capacity (cups, pints, quarts, gallons, liters). b. Length (miles, kilometers) c. Mass (ounces, pounds, grams, kilograms). d. Temperature (Fahrenheit, Celsius).	√
M9	Math	3.01	Use appropriate vocabulary to compare, describe, and classify two- and three-dimensional figures.	√

Reference Number	Subject	NC ID#	Description of Standard (Course Concept)	Used
M10	Math	3.02	Use a rectangular coordinate system to solve problems. a. Graph and identify points with whole number and/or letter coordinates. b. Describe the path between given points on the plane.	✓
M11	Math	4.01	Collect, organize, analyze, and display data (including circle graphs and tables) to solve problems.	✓
M12	Math	4.02	Determine the number of permutations and combinations of up to three items.	✓
M13	Math	4.03	Solve probability problems using permutations and combinations.	✓
M14	Math	5.01	Describe and extend numeric and geometric patterns.	✓
M15	Math	5.02	Extend and find missing terms of repeating and growing patterns.	✓
M16	Math	5.03	Use symbols to represent unknown quantities in number sentences.	✓
M17	Math	5.04	Find the value of the unknown in a number sentence.	✓
SCIENCE				
Skills in this subject area have a check in the last column if they are addressed in the book				
S1	Science	1.01	Observe and measure how the quantities and qualities of nutrients, light, and water in the environment affect plant growth.	✓
S2	Science	1.02	Observe and describe how environmental conditions determine how well plants survive and grow in a particular environment.	✓
S3	Science	1.03	Investigate and describe how plants pass through distinct stages in their life cycle including: growth, survival, reproduction.	✓
S4	Science	1.04	Explain why the number of seeds a plant produces depends on variables such as light, water, nutrients, and pollination.	✓
S5	Science	1.05	Observe and discuss how bees pollinate flowers.	✓
S6	Science	1.06	Observe, describe and record properties of germinating seeds.	✓

Reference Number	Subject	NC ID#	Description of Standard (Course Concept)	Used
S7	Science	2.01	Observe and describe the properties of soil: color, texture, capacity to hold water.	√
S8	Science	2.02	Investigate and observe that different soils absorb water at different rates.	√
S9	Science	2.03	Determine the ability of soil to support the growth of many plants, including those important to our food supply.	√
S10	Science	2.04	Identify the basic components of soil: sand, clay, humus.	√
S11	Science	2.05	Determine how composting can be used to recycle discarded plant and animal material.	√
S12	Science	2.06	Determine the relationship between heat and decaying plant matter in a compost pile.	√
S13	Science	3.01	Observe that light travels in a straight line until it strikes an object and is reflected and/or absorbed.	√
S14	Science	3.02	Observe that objects in the sky have patterns of movement including: sun, moon, stars.	√
S15	Science	3.03	Using shadows, follow and record the apparent movement of the sun in the sky during the day.	√
S16	Science	3.04	Use appropriate tools to make observations of the moon.	√
S17	Science	3.05	Observe and record the change in the apparent shape of the moon from day to day over several months and describe the pattern of changes.	√
S18	Science	3.06	Observe that patterns of stars in the sky stay the same, although they appear to move across the sky nightly.	√
S19	Science	4.01	Identify the skeleton as a system of the human body.	√
S20	Science	4.02	Describe several functions of bones: support, protection, locomotion.	√
S21	Science	4.03	Describe the functions of different types of joints: hinge, ball and socket, gliding.	√
S22	Science	4.04	Describe how different kinds of joints allow movement and compare this to the movement of mechanical devices.	√

Reference Number	Subject	NC ID#	Description of Standard (Course Concept)	Used
S23	Science	4.05	Observe and describe how muscles cause the body to move	√

SOCIAL STUDIES				
Skills in this subject area have a check in the last column if they are addressed in the book				
SS1	Social Studies	1.01	Identify and demonstrate characteristics of responsible citizenship and explain how citizen participation can impact changes within a community.	√
SS2	Social Studies	1.02	Recognize diverse local, state, and national leaders, past and present, who demonstrate responsible citizenship.	√
SS3	Social Studies	1.03	Identify and explain the importance of civic responsibility, including but not limited to, obeying laws and voting.	√
SS4	Social Studies	1.04	Explain the need for leaders in communities and describe their roles and responsibilities.	√
SS5	Social Studies	1.05	Suggest responsible courses of action in given situations and assess the consequences of irresponsible behavior.	√
SS6	Social Studies	1.06	Identify selected personalities associated with major holidays and cultural celebrations.	√
SS7	Social Studies	2.01	Distinguish and compare economic and social roles of children and adults in the local community to selected communities around the world.	√
SS8	Social Studies	2.02	Analyze similarities and differences among families in different times and in different places.	√
SS9	Social Studies	2.03	Describe similarities and differences among communities in different times and in different places.	√
SS10	Social Studies	3.01	Analyze changes, which have occurred in communities past and present.	√
SS11	Social Studies	3.02	Describe how individuals, events, and ideas change over time.	√
SS12	Social Studies	3.03	Compare and contrast the family structure and the roles of its members over time.	√
SS13	Social Studies	4.01	Distinguish between various types of maps and globes.	√
SS14	Social Studies	4.02	Use appropriate source maps to locate communities.	√

Reference Number	Subject	NC ID#	Description of Standard (Course Concept)	Used
SS15	Social Studies	4.03	Use geographic terminology to describe and explain variations in the physical environment as communities.	✓
SS16	Social Studies	4.04	Compare how people in different communities adapt to or modify the physical environment to meet their needs.	✓
SS17	Social Studies	5.01	Define and identify examples of scarcity.	✓
SS18	Social Studies	5.02	Explain the impact of scarcity on the production, distribution, and consumption of goods and services.	✓
SS19	Social Studies	5.03	Apply concepts of specialization and division of labor to the local community.	✓
SS20	Social Studies	5.04	Compare and contrast the division of labor in local and global communities.	✓
SS21	Social Studies	5.05	Distinguish and analyze the economic resources within communities.	✓
SS22	Social Studies	5.06	Recognize and explain reasons for economic interdependence of communities.	✓
SS23	Social Studies	5.07	Identify historic figures and leaders who have influenced the economies of communities and evaluate the effectiveness of their contributions.	✓
SS24	Social Studies	6.01	Describe and assess ways in which technology is used in a community's economy.	✓
SS25	Social Studies	6.02	Identify and describe contributions made by community leaders in technology.	✓
SS26	Social Studies	6.03	Identify the impact of technological change on communities around the world.	✓
SS27	Social Studies	7.01	Identify the deeds of local and global leaders.	✓
SS28	Social Studies	7.02	Assess the heroic deeds of characters from folktales and legends.	✓
SS29	Social Studies	7.03	Explore the role of selected fictional characters in creating new communities.	✓

* Standards are not taught to mastery. In some cases, standards are simply identified, and it is up to the teacher or parent to use the teachable moment to further expand on the standard. Visit http://www.chickennuggetman.com/standards for an updated version of this standards table, which changes when the Department of Public Instruction revises the curriculum.

** In some cases, questions correlate to more than one Bloom's Taxonomy level.